P9-BIE-387

ΛΛΛΙΠ
ΜΡ 14/18

FLIGHT OF THE OUTCAST

theacademy:year1

brad strickland

sourcebooks
jabberwocky

Copyright © 2010 by Brad Strickland
Cover and internal design © 2010 by Sourcebooks, Inc.
Cover design by Gothamhaus Design
Cover images © snez_4eva/iStockphoto.com; Emin Ozkan/Shutterstock.com; Tim Paterson/Flickr.com

Sourcebooks and the colophon are registered trademarks of Sourcebooks, Inc.

All rights reserved. No part of this book may be reproduced in any form or by any electronic or mechanical means including information storage and retrieval systems—except in the case of brief quotations embodied in critical articles or reviews—without permission in writing from its publisher, Sourcebooks, Inc.

The characters and events portrayed in this book are fictitious or are used fictitiously. Any similarity to real persons, living or dead, is purely coincidental and not intended by the author.

Published by Sourcebooks Jabberwocky, an imprint of Sourcebooks, Inc.
P.O. Box 4410, Naperville, Illinois 60567-4410
(630) 961-3900
Fax: (630) 961-2168
www.jabberwockykids.com

Library of Congress Cataloging-in-Publication Data

Strickland, Brad.
  Flight of the Outcast : the Academy, year 1 / by Brad Strickland.
    p. cm.
  Summary: When thirteen-year-old Asteria's family is killed by space raiders, she leaves their farm on the fringe planet Theron and uses her desire for revenge as motivation at the Royal Military Academy, where she is treated as a second-class citizen because of her father's unfairly stained reputation.
  (pbk. : alk. paper) [1. Science fiction. 2. Schools—Fiction. 3. Social classes—Fiction. 4. Revenge—Fiction. 5. Orphans—Fiction.] I. Title.
  PZ7.S9166Fli 2010
  [Fic]—dc22
                        2009049924

Source of Production: Versa Press, East Peoria, Illinois, USA
Date of Production: April 2010
Run Number: 12242

Printed and bound in the United States of America.
VP 10 9 8 7 6 5 4 3 2 1

part 1

the attack

ONE

Asteria Locke's world ended quite suddenly one noon in the early summer of her thirteenth Standard year. Before that hour, she had been the daughter of a farmer on the fringe planet of Theron. Before that day, she had no brothers or sisters, but she did have a cousin who—how she envied him—had been destined to travel offworld, to study at the most prestigious school in the Empyrion. She also had a father who had once served in the Royal Empyrean Space Fleet, though her mother had been dead for a long time.

After that day, she had no one.

Yet after that day—after that hour—she set out on the long path to becoming a legend.

It all ended, and it all started, on her father's Upland farm on Frejaland, the northernmost continent of Theron. Asteria thought of it as a crowded land. It held nearly seventy thousand humans in all, counting the three who lived on the farm.

The farm perched on the high plateau called Keleran. The soil there was fertile. Carlson Locke had always told his daughter they were lucky the Empyrion had given them forty thousand hectares of such land to farm. There he had built a home, raised biodomes, become a prosperous farmer—and had married a wife and fathered one child, a girl, Asteria.

Who was currently bored out of her mind.

Asteria Locke wondered for the thousandth time why her father refused to purchase Cybots to help on the farm. Or why he would not trust the Artificial Intelligence machinery to do its job on its own. Instead he insisted that she and her cousin, Andre, help him with the crops. So here she sat in the cockpit of a massive crawling crop tender, wishing she were somewhere else. Or at least wishing for a surprise visit from her dad, spanking new Cybot in tow, to run the AI. Her wrist transceiver chirped, and she said, "Yes, Dad?"

Carlson Locke's crisp voice asked, "Where are you, Star?"

Star. Asteria wrinkled her nose at the babyish nickname. "I'm in Dome Seven. Where else would I—"

The connection broke.

"Checking up on me," muttered Asteria. You'd think he'd know that a thirteen-year-old was responsible enough to do the job without his constant micromanagement. But no. Probably came of his experience in the Royal Space Fleet. Everything had to be shipshape and military style.

The crop tender slowly rolled along, its tires (taller than she was) sticking precisely in the furrows between the plants. The pliant, flexible green blades of the coffera crop—the grain so nutritious that it made colonization of nearly barren worlds possible—folded forward under the rollers of the machine, to be scanned, evaluated, checked for parasites, and then fertilized and watered to exact specifications.

Asteria gazed up at the vast expanse of glass above her. She might as well have been fifty kilometers away…or fifty light years, for that matter. Her brain was meant for more than farming.

The high agridome was necessary, because on the Keleran Plateau, the growing season otherwise would have been short and brutally cool. The structure was so huge that she could see a drift of cloud just below the far-off ceiling. When the crops were nearing harvest, the domes became humid, and occasionally, the clouds produced a thin indoor rain, drifting down lazily in the low gravity of this world. Outside the domes waist-deep fangrass waved in chilly breezes, flashing silver and scarlet. Outside the sky overhead was deep blue, etched with streaky ice clouds. Inside, though, the air felt almost muggy.

All the readouts continued to be nominal. Hoping her father wasn't monitoring her too closely, Asteria plugged in a pulsebook. She shivered as the neural connection sent first a cold, then a warm feeling flooding down her spine. Then the book took over, and she let herself relax into the near-trance state that she loved so much. In a burst, the pulsebook planted the new chapter in her mind. It would flower not only in words but in sights, sounds, smells, and tastes. The book would become as real in her mind as a memory. It was a history book. She was up to Chapter 11, which told of the Empyrion's first encounter with the Tetras, the alien race that still posed a threat somewhere out there in the vastness of the galaxy.

In the two-thousand-and-first year of the Empyrion, under the rule of the Dantor Dynasty, the Royal Military Academy received as its priority mission the discovery and settling of additional colony worlds. The first of these were the Varrian Cluster planets, the seven worlds most like the lost home planet of Earth, with the correct balance of oxygen and water. Tolerable temperature ranges permitted—

With her eyes closed, Asteria skipped ahead. She knew all the dry background stuff already. She wanted to see the battle.

...as the Third Exploratory Fleet dropped into normal space just outside the Vigan System, for the first time humans came under attack.

In her mind's eye the massacre unreeled: The human ships were enormous, six craft in all, each carrying a complement of more than a thousand people. They looked like scale-model planets, dully gleaming silver spheres bristling with instruments and weapons.

The Tetraploid ships that assaulted them were tiny slivers by comparison: silvery spearheads so small that not even a tiny human could fit inside them. They darted in at incredible speeds, fired their weapons mercilessly—and when the human crafts' shields held, they rammed the much larger vessels. The first few impacted the shields and exploded. The following alien craft slowed until they were able to penetrate the force barrier. Whoever controlled them seemed to realize that projectiles and missiles moving at top speed were held back, but anything going slower than a thousand kilometers a second could break through.

When the small alien ships came in contact with the hulls, they exploded. The tiny, fiery eruptions made Asteria wince as the human ships—the *Cancarra, Apex, Strigia,* and *Hosmer*—blasted apart silently, one by one. The remaining two human vessels, the *Concord* and the *Svestia,* attempted to escape into translight space. Only the *Svestia* made it. She limped back to port with a third of her crew dead or wounded to report that for the very first time in history, humanity had encountered hostile aliens.

The Space Fleet immediately began to create a counter-strike force—

Asteria's communicator chirped again, rousing her from her reverie. "Yes, Dad?"

"Home. Now. Raiders."

Raiders.

Asteria's initial reaction upon hearing the word was numb shock. Then she felt as if an ice-cold hand had suddenly grasped her insides. Her mother had died in a Raider attack. Raiders were why Carlson Locke had insisted on building weapons towers, never once used—until now. "What do we—?"

"Home. I've alerted Andre. Run!"

Asteria swung out of the cockpit, kicked wide, and dropped down into the green shadows of the plants. She landed lightly and ran toward the air lock at racing speed—a small advantage of living on a planet with .88 normal gravity but training in a gym adjusted to 1.02 normal. The drooping blades whipped against her cheeks. Before she had run the half-kilometer to the triple air lock, her chest was heaving. She grimaced, knowing what waited for her.

She took a deep breath and hurried outside. The air, thin and cold at this altitude, burned her lungs. Midsummer, and the temperature outside the domes was only eleven degrees. A flicker of bitter resentment mingled with her fear. Showed you how grateful the Empyrion was: give a hero a huge spread of land on the cold and barren heights of a third-rate planet on the far edge of civilization—

Asteria gasped, hoping for her second wind. The farm now had nine domes, having added the newest one at the end of the last growing season, and she was far from the house. It was a long run. At least it was downhill—the fall line lay only a few kilometers south of the house, and then the land dropped dramatically down to sea level. There, the nearest town, Sanctal, clustered along the narrow flatlands at the mouth of a fjord.

She caught a glimpse of a figure, lean and lanky, running too. "Andre!" Asteria gasped, and her cousin drew up short.

"I've got to get to the defensive tower," he choked out, his eyes wide.

"Has Dad called Sanctal for help?"

"Sanctal?" he spat. "You know what they call us: Unbelievers. No help from them, not against Raiders. I've got to go!"

He ran like a gazelle in the low gravity. Asteria, winded, all but stumbled to the house air lock. Her father waited for her, his face hard as though chiseled from stone. "Hurry. They'll be here within minutes." His cybernetic left eye glared red at her. His cybernetic left hand reached out, seized her arm, and dragged her into the lock. "I want you to go to the shelter. Andre's manning the north defensive tower. I'll take the south. I'll call you when it's all clear." His scarred face was grim below the mop of shaggy brown hair. In Sanctal, his stitched-together face, with its artificial eye, attracted shocked stares. But Asteria had never known anything different. He looked the way a dad should look—even when his red eye gazed balefully at her.

"I'll fight," gasped Asteria as the warmer, pressurized air inside the house filled her lungs. "I can take the particle cannon—"

Carlson Locke shook his head, jerking his square chin to the side in curt refusal. "No. I want you in the shelter."

"Dad, I won't go!" The volume of her own voice surprised her.

"I'm sorry, Star."

She didn't register the weapon in his hand until he had thumbed the trigger. She tried to yell a protest, but the stasis beam hit her, and she felt her muscles seize. Awareness dimmed as her father easily lifted her and carried her down a flight of steps through a long, arched corridor, with the lights overhead flicking on. At the far end, he paused as the vault door's AI recognized him and opened up.

The shelter was the only shielded room on the farmstead— shielding was a costly energy sink—and it was not only the theoretical retreat in case of attack, but where Carlson stored anything valuable. He laid Asteria down on a cot that folded out of the wall and stroked her hair. "I'll come back when it's all clear." His voice was gruff but tender.

That was the last she heard from him. It was the last time she felt his touch.

She sank into unconsciousness. The pulsebook chapter reactivated in her dreaming mind, and she saw the horrific First Battle of the Varrian Cluster unreeling in her dreams. The destruction overwhelmed her.

* * *

At some point she felt a tremendous seismic jolt. In her dreaming mind, the sensation coincided with the destruction of the barren Third Moon of Helis, the Tetra base that had cost the lives of nearly a million humans in the battles that raged in the Varrian Cluster over the first hundred years of the Tetra Wars. Part of her concentrated on the familiar history lesson, while another part desperately warned her to *wake up, wake up, wake up—*

Slowly she fought her way back to consciousness and switched off the pulsebook replay with a flicker of thought. She could move her head, rolling it from side to side. Her mouth was bone dry, her tongue like a raspy block of wood.

"Dad?" It came out as a frog-croak.

Asteria focused on recovering from the lingering effects of the stasis beam. She lay in darkness. Her shoulders could move a little. She rocked. The room detected the movement, and the lights came on—the dim red emergency lights. Something was wrong.

A painful tingling flooded into arms and legs, hands and feet. She managed to sit up. "Water," she gasped.

A wall panel opened. She pushed herself up and staggered to it. Water flowed, and she stooped to lap it up. It was tepid, not cool as it should have been. Didn't matter. Tasted wonderful. Her tongue began to feel normal again. She cleared her throat and activated her wrist transceiver. "Dad?"

No answer. "Andre? Talk to me!"

Her cousin didn't respond. Maybe he had switched off his transceiver. He was almost the same age as she was, only three Standard months older, but he got away with things that Carlson would have punished her for. When she thought she could walk—even though the floor felt as if it were heaving slowly, like the deck of a ship on a rolling sea—Asteria made her way to the vault door, leaning on the wall along the way. "Open."

Nothing happened.

"Open!" Asteria commanded in a louder voice.

The door remained locked. Groaning, Asteria reached for the access hatch. From inside she could open the door manually, but it was difficult. She tugged at the spoked wheel of the emergency release, her shoulders straining and sweat popping out on her forehead. The door creaked back, centimeter by centimeter.

Acrid gray smoke streamed through the opening, bringing tears to Asteria's eyes and making her cough. She dropped to her hands and knees and looked out through the narrow space.

Darkness. Asteria stood, leaned against the door with her shoulder until it closed again, and hoped the air system was still working well enough to clean up the smoke. She needed more light. She opened lockers, searching. She found the financial and legal documents her father had stored; she found holopics and recordings of her mother, who had died when Asteria was only four. In the third locker, she discovered a kind of belt, made of thin metallic plates. She had never seen it before. The plates were as large as her hands, shiny and curiously light, as if they had hardly any substance to them. Yet the belt felt tough and flexible. She experimentally looped it around her waist—it was much too large to fit her—and felt a flash of surprise as she touched the two ends together and they joined, and the belt tightened, not uncomfortably but snugly. She couldn't find the release, so she moved on.

Finally, she opened a locker that held, among other things, a powerful flashlight. She retrieved it, went back to the door, and grunted as she manually opened it again. The smoke seemed less dense this time, but still, she dropped to her knees as she shone the light out the narrow opening she had made.

Her breath came up short.

The corridor ended abruptly a few meters ahead. It had caved in. She was trapped. Gray tendrils of smoke curled like

11

lazy cobras on the ceiling of the shattered corridor. The air stank of burned circuits.

Despite the smoke that stung her eyes, she could see a few shafts of sunlight near the ceiling. Maybe she could force her way out.

She clambered up the chunks of fallen stone and metal, cutting her palm on something sharp. At the top, she shoved until some of the rubble fell away. The smoke streamed out, and hacking miserably, with tears running down her face, Asteria wormed through the opening she had made.

Oh my—

A muted cry escaped her lips. The farmhouse was…gone. It looked as though it had been hit with a particle bomb. Nothing but charred wreckage remained. The corridor had led from the house entrance way down to four meters beneath the surface, then twenty-five meters away from the house. Now it was at the surface, on the edge of a shallow rubble-filled bowl. The north and south defensive towers had been reduced to broken stubs.

"Dad?" Asteria said in a trembling voice. "Andre?"

As though in answer, she heard a far-off growl. Dome 1, the only one with a ripe crop, had been blasted open. A ship climbed away from it on a pillar of fire.

Asteria stood in shock. The Raider ship became a speck in the sky.

"Father," she said softly. And then she cried aloud, "Father!"

Yet even as she cried out, she knew he was no longer there to answer her.

two

Asteria was desperately clearing rubble from the smoking pile that had been the south defensive tower—searching for any sign of her family—when the battered hovercart roared up the steep road from Sanctal. Two men emerged. They wore the drab, dark gray coveralls of the lower-caste Bourse. She stood holding a stone as they walked toward her, their faces grim.

"What happened?" one asked. "There was a distress call."

"And you came," she said bitterly. "The two of you."

The second man pointed at the shattered dome. "Raiders."

"May Shayman, the god of protection, favor us," the first one said.

Asteria felt like hitting him with the stone. "My father and my cousin—"

"Please." The second man took the stone from her hand and said, "The Cybots will search for them better than we can. Come. We will take you to safety."

Asteria shook her head. "I want to stay here."

"Child," the first man said, "Gaiam, the god of family, tells us we must take in the young of—" His voice seemed to falter. "Of those who have met with accidents."

"I don't believe in your gods," she snapped, and the two men exchanged a shocked look.

"If your people are alive, the Cybots will find them," the second man told her.

"They're not alive," Asteria said bleakly.

The first man said, "If they are not, we will take care of you."

She hated them. *Hated* them. But at last, with nowhere to go, she let them take her to Sanctal. They sped back down toward the seacoast town, the smoldering farm vanishing over the rim of the plateau. The air grew warmer and smelled of the sea. They slowed as they entered the town, and people stared at her. The outsider. The orphan. The outcast. Asteria stared back defiantly, holding back her tears. She went where the men took her, answered the questions the Bourse magistrate put to her, and did not object when he turned her over to a woman who said she would take Asteria to a place where she could live until a decision might be reached concerning her future.

Asteria did not object to any of this. But already she was thinking of her future. Of revenge.

* * *

For many days, Asteria felt like a prisoner, even though she had all the freedom that an Unbeliever girl was allowed in Sanctal. She could walk around the narrow streets of the settlement—if she had a male escort. She could speak to anyone—if the other person spoke first. They dressed her in the drab clothing of a Sanctal subclass girl: gray cap and tunic, dark gray stockings, black shoes. They complained about the belt: "Ornaments are signs of pride. That is not acceptable to Drakkah, the god of humility. Remove it."

"I can't!" she'd snapped repeatedly. And she couldn't. The flexible belt had almost molded itself to her waist. It was loose enough for her to remove her clothes, but when she put on the Sanctal garb, she had to put it on over the belt, which now lay snugly against her skin. It didn't seem to have any kind of release. Asteria had never seen anything like it. She couldn't imagine what it was supposed to be—or do.

After two days, the Cybots sent by the Bourse returned with the meager items they had found: the ID and communicator elements from both Carlson and Andre Locke's wrist transceivers. They had discovered these in the ruins of the defensive towers—along with enough bone fragments to identify the bodies of both Asteria's father and her cousin.

Asteria told the sour-faced Bourse officials that the killers had been Raiders, renegades. That they should be pursued, caught, and punished. The Bourse never made a decision without debate; it was the core of their religious law, though they allowed no debate when it came to their beliefs. Hour after hour, they sat arguing about what they should do. In the end, they decided to apply for help to the planetary governor, whose offices were a thousand miles to the south, in the large settlement of Central. That took a day. And then Baron Kamedes, the ultimate authority on Theron, sent back word that the death of the Lockes was a local issue. The Bourse should handle everything.

All that debate for nothing, Asteria thought bitterly as she sat in the solitary cell they had prepared for her in their holding center for orphans and strays.

And so the Bourse did handle everything. Slowly. The day following the governor's decision was the Holy Day of Repentance, when Bourse settlers remained shut in rooms thinking of their sins. Nothing could be done. Then came the Day of Appeal, on which Bourse men and women flocked to the various temples of the gods and prayed for whatever they needed. Old men went to the Temple of Prosperity. Young men went to the Temple of Love. Women went to the Temple of Patience or the Temple of Endurance. Asteria sat alone in the little room they had provided and grew more and more frustrated.

At last, long after the raid, the local council sat in conference to decide Asteria's fate. She was not allowed to speak, though the Bourse granted her an advocate—a lean, grim-faced man of thirty named Nels. Six elders, clad in black and looking as solemn as attendees at a funeral, sat on a high platform behind an imposing wooden table carved in figures of dour saints, and listened as the case director, a grizzled old man named Marren, laid out the facts.

The head of the panel of elders summed up: "So this infidel girl is left without a family? And she is heir to the estate?"

"That is the case, my masters," said old Marren.

Asteria could see greed flickering in the elderly eyes. Sanctal was a place where people who believed in simplicity and devotion could live and pursue their vision of the holy life. But forty thousand hectares of land, with seven intact and functioning biodomes producing a rich crop of coffera…well, that was a solemn thought indeed. If the farm could continue, even with only seven domes working, it could produce enough income to appeal to a family.

"She must be given to a husband," the elder at the far end of the table said, looking down at Asteria. "She looks to be sturdy enough. She must learn our ways and our beliefs and become one of us. She must learn to serve the Six Great Gods of the Bourse."

"All glory to the gods," the others murmured ritualistically.

"I don't want—" began Asteria hotly, but Nels shushed her.

"My masters," he said, rising, "the girl is not yet sixteen Standard. In three years' time, she may be of age to be married, but now our laws forbid that."

Marren shrugged. "Then she must be fostered into a family of believers," he said simply. "There she may be disciplined and schooled and brought to a knowledge of her place in serving the gods."

Asteria again saw those flickers of interest. A foster family might have the inside track. And the income from the farm would be put in trust for the lucky husband, but some of it would go to the foster family. It would be profitable to be the guardian of a girl who would inherit a freehold of land.

"That is a good point," the chairman of the council said. "It would be well for her to learn proper manners and behavior. She must learn that she cannot speak out of turn, for one thing. She seems a headstrong, willful girl, and we could not accept her into our fold unless she learned to curb that haughty spirit."

"My master," said the elder to the chairman's left, a thin-faced old man with a fringe of white beard. "If you will permit, I think my eldest son, Kern, might take her in. He farms too, but not in the Uplands. He has a boy about her age—"

A man on the other side of the chairman cut in, "With submission, my master, I believe that our family could provide the girl with a better grounding in our beliefs. We live in the town, sir, and not out in the country. 'Many eyes make good behavior,' so say the gods."

"So say the gods," the group chanted, without missing a beat.

The man continued. "In our family, we could always keep a close watch—"

"Sirs," said Nels, standing beside Asteria. "Masters, please. This is a matter for a full council meeting. May we not defer this until the next session? Is it not enough today to decide that Asteria Locke is to become a ward of the Bourse, to be molded into a suitable wife and companion for a Bourse son, and to allot her a portion of the income from her father's farm for her temporary support?"

"The young man has a good point," said the chairman. "'Haste spills the water,' as it is written."

"As it is written," the group chanted.

"Are all in agreement?" the chairman asked. "Then it is thus decreed: the girl will continue to live in the Hospitality Hall, and her food, clothing, and other necessities are to be paid for from the proceeds of the farm."

Asteria leaped to her feet. "What about the Raiders?" she yelled.

It was as if she were a ghost. No one even reacted to her. Nels pulled her back down into her chair, not harshly but firmly. He said, "My masters, the girl would like to know if any steps are being taken to punish the Raiders."

"Tell her," said the chairman gravely, "that such events are manifestations of Balzius, the god of fate."

Asteria said fiercely, "Then are my father's murderers to escape without punishment?"

Finally, the chairman took notice of her. He sternly said, "Punishment and reward are not for human wills or hands to disperse. The Empyrion maintains protection over our world; it is up to the Empyrion to pursue those who have killed her family. They mind the worldly business, and the Bourse mind the more important business of the soul. Is there anything else?"

Fiercely, Asteria whispered into Nels's ear. He straightened and said, "My masters, the girl would like the personal possessions and the legal documents taken by the Cybots from the ruins of her home. Is that permitted?"

More murmuring consultation among the men on the bench. Then the chairman said firmly, "She must learn that mere material things of this world are no longer of any importance. However, for the time being, recognizing the tragedy of her experience, we will permit her to select six items to retain. The rest will be kept safely for the man who will eventually marry her." He stood. "It is so decided. May our decision please the Six Great Gods."

The others droned, "All glory to the gods—"

But Asteria was no longer even listening.

* * *

Six things to represent her whole life. Because the Bourse believed that the gods ordained six as the perfect number, she could choose only six.

A picture of her father and her cousin, Andre—dark-haired like her, blue-eyed like her, laughing in the image. She cried a little. She and Andre had been such a handful, always practicing martial arts when they should have been working. Andre, always boasting of his appointment to the Royal Military Academy in Corona, the capital of the Empyrion. She, always envious that he was to be released from the dull world of Theron, from the boring farm.

She would give anything to be back on that farm now.

Another picture, her mother, whom she barely remembered. Felice Locke had been a willowy thing, a sixth-generation inhabitant of a low-gravity planet. She had been a supervising technician during her husband's many operations and slow recuperation. She had married Carlson Locke before he had received his pension and land grant, before he had become prosperous. Her mother had known that her health was fragile, that childbirth would weaken her, and yet she had given birth to Asteria. She had been ill in Sanctal the last time Raiders had attacked, and when their bombs collapsed part of the hospital, she had perished.

Four more. Asteria kept the land-grant deed, her cousin's ID/ communicator processor, a digitized copy of her father's will (leaving everything to her), and an old-fashioned paper document. It was only a few tens of centimeters square, and it did include an embedded chip that validated its information.

Asteria read the dust-smudged letters:

KNOW ALL BY THIS CERTIFICATE

In recognition for the service rendered by Carlson Locke to the Royal Space Fleet, the Empyrion grants to A. F. Locke the privilege of attending the Royal Military Academy when said candidate reaches the age of thirteen Standard years.

Asteria's middle name was Felice, after her mother. Andre's had been Fredric, after his maternal grandfather.

They were both A. F. Locke.

In the privacy of her room at the Hospitality Hall—a bare cubical with only a bed, a chair, a desk, and walls that continually glowed with shifting religious texts—Asteria thought about what she was going to do.

It was illegal.

There would be trouble.

But she would face the trouble when it came, and it would come when she was far away from this place.

At least the Bourse ignored her for the most part. It would be almost comical, if it weren't so nightmarish. They seemed afraid that her lack of belief in their Six Great Gods might be contagious. Except for mealtimes, she could be on her own for most of every day—as long as she didn't want to do something that girls were not permitted to do, like go outside.

The Hospitality Hall, Asteria thought, could not be much different from a Bourse prison. It was a long, low building constructed of blocks of gray stone quarried from the fjord cliffs. The rooms were tiny and dark, each with only one small square window. The Bourse had put Asteria in a room far down from the only door. She had no neighbors. Three times a day, a Cybot brought food, and the travelers who stayed at the Hospitality House ate at a table in the center of the building.

The Cybot seated Asteria all by herself, at a small table in a dark nook. No one particularly noticed her. Once a woman wearing the small, red flame tattoo of the Aristocracy took a meal in the Hospitality Hall. Asteria glimpsed her, surrounded by servants, but Asteria wasn't even allowed to eat in the same room as an Aristo. The Cybot brought her meal to her room.

21

It looked like a slender robot, approximately human-shaped, with a tiny head that was mostly binocular eyes (they glowed red, like her father's artificial one had) and a smaller triangular sensor array. The arms were capable of complex bends, not like a man's arm, and the hands were very delicate.

"Who are you?" Asteria asked it as it served her bread, water, and a thin vegetable soup.

"Unit 2312 Th-301," the Cybot said in a soft, uninflected voice.

"Who were you when you were human?"

"That question has no meaning for me."

No, of course not. Cybots had portions of functioning human brains at their core—but brains stripped of personality and memory. No Cybot remembered its former identity. None of them had emotions. Most of them had the brains of condemned criminals in their chest cavities. If the Raiders who had killed her family were captured alive, this would be their fate. They would live on in a way—unconsciously, to be sure—for perhaps two hundred Standard years as the central intelligence units of Cybots. Asteria knew all this, but because her father refused to deal with Cybots—he thought that their very creation was cruel—she had never had a chance to speak to one before.

"Do you have to accept my orders?" asked Asteria.

"I must perform any lawful activity commanded by a human," responded the Cybot.

"I want a faulty transceiving unit replaced," she said.

"I am capable of performing that action."

"Here, then."

It took less than a minute. The Cybot unquestioningly removed the central unit from her wrist transceiver and replaced it with the one she supplied. It then asked, "Do you require initialization?"

"No!" The word came out more quickly and anxiously than she had intended. She strapped the transceiver onto her wrist. "This one has been pre-programmed. Uh, thank you. Don't tell anyone about this."

"Unless my directives are overridden. Do you require anything more?"

"That will do," Asteria said. "Thank you."

The Cybot stared at her. "'Thank you' has no meaning to me."

* * *

She was not exactly a prisoner. Yet if she started toward the outer door of the Hall, started to walk forth in the streets of Sanctal, immediately someone would stop her: "Maiden, you cannot walk alone. Back into the Hall, or find an escort."

And so she became a thief and an impostor. A young man, hardly taller or heavier than she was, unexpectedly spoke to her one lunchtime: "Child, can you name the Six Principles of Good Living?"

"I'm not a Bourse," she said, but not harshly. She was studying the thin, young fellow's black-and-white tunic and baggy, gray trousers. "Sir, are you a priest?"

The young fellow actually blushed. "I am an apprentice priest of Hippock, the god of healing," he said. "I have been sent by our settlement to learn medical arts here at the House of Healing."

"My name is Asteria Locke."

"I am Harst Gavron." He cleared his throat. "So you are an Unbeliever? I have never met one."

"Would you like to tell me about the six gods?" she asked innocently. "Do you have time? Are you staying here or just having a meal?"

"Oh, I'm staying," he said. "The third room there."

"It's small and dark, isn't it?" Asteria said.

He looked eager. "Oh, plainness is a virtue! 'A man's spirit flourishes if his life is spare.' So say the gods."

Asteria nodded.

His gaze grew intense. "So say the gods," he repeated.

Suddenly she understood that he expected her to chant the words along with him. She couldn't bring herself to do it, so she just shrugged.

The poor young man spent the next hour telling her how good discomfort was for the soul. And when he left the Hospitality Hall for the Hall of Healing, she gave him the chance to experience a little more of that wonderful discomfort. She slipped into his room and stole his only other tunic and trousers—and hid them well before calling the Cybot in to her little room.

"Cut my hair," she told it. "Cut it very short."

The Cybot obeyed, trimming her hair so close to her skull so only a dark mist seemed to cling to it. A little later, in the cool twilight, she went out dressed as a young priest, carrying almost nothing with her.

No one seemed to notice her.

Sanctal clung to the southern shore of the fjord. It was a twisting, narrow town with three parallel streets crammed onto the little, flat shelf that backed against the high, dark crags behind. But what the town lacked in depth it made up for in length: it followed the jagged lines of the fjord for many kilometers. The dwellings looked as though they'd sprung from the rocky ground—all of them low, their walls made of the gray stone and their roofs of black slate. Everything looked wet even in dry weather.

Asteria tried to remember the town's geography from the times she had come in with her father to deliver crops or to bargain for supplies. She knew where one vital spot was—the landing center. It was far up the fjord, on a kind of plateau overlooking the town. She made her way toward it, following a winding street. At one point, she could look seaward through a narrow cleft in the cliffs and see the dark rolling ocean. At another, she could not even see the Sound, the harbor around which the town clustered. She climbed, heading inland and upward, wondering when the people at the Hospitality Hall would miss her.

At last, she saw the high force-wall pylons ahead. Out of breath, she trudged up the last incline to the gate. A heavyset man in the black and silver uniform of an Empyrean guard sat in a security booth. He looked bored. "Business?" he asked.

"I want to find a ship to take me offworld," she said, trying to pitch her voice low.

The guard laughed. "Eager to get off this rock pile? There's only the shuttle to the high docks. It leaves in a little less than a Standard hour. Departure pads are to your left. It will be Station One."

It didn't take her long to find the small ship, poised to spring. She spoke to a crewman, who took her to the captain, a worried-looking man well into middle age. His cheek tattoo was tiny and on the left cheek—he was an Aristo, but one of a minor branch. "Passage to the high docks?" he asked. "That's expensive."

"This trip is on the Empyrion," she said. She showed him the document.

He scowled at it, then scanned her wrist transceiver. His scanner spoke to him: "A. F. Locke, candidate cadet for the Royal Military Academy. All ships are directed to assist this candidate cadet to secure passage to Corona."

The captain frowned. "The Empyrion reimbursement won't even cover the extra fuel cost."

"Scan this," she said, producing the datacard that held the details of her inheritance. He did and looked at her with more respect.

"I'll make out an order to pay you from that," she said.

"All right—*sonny*," the captain said with a wry look. "At least I'll get the Empyrion payment. Climb aboard." His voice fell to a whisper. "And don't trust that haircut to fool everybody."

Wincing in irritation at her own timidity, Asteria turned away and hurried toward the boarding ladder. An Aristocrat could order a Commoner to be arrested without a warrant, impris-oned with no charges—and she was a Commoner: a Commoner whose disguise had just been compromised, no less.

But still, she had an appointment to the Royal Military Academy, she reminded herself. She climbed a steep ladder through an open hatchway. The interior of the shuttle was dim, and it smelled of sweat. A double row of seats ran down a short passageway, arranged back to back. Twenty seats in all, no one in any of them. She went to the far end, sat down, and strapped herself in.

There was a flurry of clangs and clatters as the shuttle prepared for takeoff. Whirs and whines of machinery. Asteria crossed her arms and sat with her chin on her chest, trying to fight the flutter of her heart. Why couldn't they just go? Why did they have to wait here on the ground? If they had missed her in the Hospitality Hall—if poor apprentice priest Harst had returned and found his spare clothing gone, if someone came looking—

After what seemed more like half a day than half an hour, the captain's voice rang out: "We are ready to lift off. Make sure your seat restraints are secure. In the event of an emergency, don't worry about a thing, because you'll die." He barked a short laugh. "Understood?"

So she was to be the only passenger. Only when the shuttle rattled, roared, tilted steeply, and surged into space did Asteria allow herself to relax. Her palms hurt from where her fingernails had clenched into them.

"So we made it out okay," the captain's voice said. "We'll dock in about fifteen minutes. Remain in your seat until I give clearance. We're in free fall, so don't try to move around."

She took a deep breath. She didn't know what would happen on the space station, the High Docks. She didn't know whether or not she could bluff her way to Corona. She'd have to work on that. Concentrate on being a boy. Being boyish, anyway. She didn't even know if she could.

But she did know, with deep certainty, that she would rather die than marry a sour, obsessive member of the Bourse. Whatever else she was, an orphan and an outcast, Asteria was free.

three

The High Docks hung in a stable orbit over Theron, so far away from the planet that it could be seen whole through the viewports. The orbit was not quite synchronous—you could see the slow turning of Theron if you were patient. Asteria had never been so far offworld before.

The station was a warren of tubes and gratings. The metal walls might once have been painted white, but now they were shades of dingy ranging from nearly black to a gruesome tan. Seen from outside, the Docks looked like an enormous wheel, rotating on its axis. From inside, it was grubby and claustrophobic. The shuttle captain had sent her to an arrival room, where a Cybot had scanned her in.

Immediately, it told her to report to the transportation officer on Level Three, Radiant Two, Office Nine. She had no idea where that was. The Cybot placed a finger to her head and in a short pulse sent her the station map.

So she knew to climb a ladder up three levels and go to a tubeway so narrow that it had recesses in the walls every ten steps—if you met someone heading your way, you could squeeze in and let the other person pass. This was one of the spokes of the wheel. It was under microgravity, so you did not walk but hauled yourself along by rungs set into the walls. It widened out again, and Asteria swung down into near-1.0 gravity, hanging by her hands for a second before dropping to the deck. Office Nine was just ahead.

The transportation officer was a woman, gray-haired and sharp-featured. "I've seen your documentation," she said in an impatient tone. "A. F. Locke, bound for Corona. Why are you wasting time here?"

"I want to wait for a ship," Asteria said.

"It'll be a week before a ship bound that way docks here. You could have checked the schedule. Where do you propose to stay?"

Asteria shrugged. "I thought I'd make do somehow. I can stay in the passenger boarding area if it comes to that."

The woman snorted. "For a week? And how are you going to eat?"

"You have rations, don't you?"

The woman sat back in her chair and brushed a stray tendril of hair from her cheek. "Do you have money to pay for your keep?"

"I have an account on the surface. In the town of Sanctal."

"In care of the Bourse?"

Asteria nodded.

Making a wry face, the woman said, "I suppose you know how easy they'll make it to collect what's due. Girl, don't you know anything?"

Asteria cringed at the word *girl*. So much for her brilliant plan.

"You're a legacy appointment to the RMA, according to your documentation," the woman continued. "Didn't your father provide you with a travel allowance account?"

"My father is dead." In a flat voice, Asteria told her of the raid, the wreck of the farm, and her decision to leave the planet as soon as she could—including her decision to disguise herself as a boy to escape the Bourse. She figured that it was best to tell the whole truth. They'd find out anyway.

"We've had no report of Raiders," the woman said, scowling.

"You wouldn't. The Bourse want to keep it quiet, and the Empyrion administrators don't seem to care—as long as they're not personally attacked."

"Let me see what I can do." The woman rose from behind her desk, told Asteria to stay put, and left her alone. Asteria slumped in her chair, glumly realizing how difficult things were going to be. She had not really thought ahead, not beyond leaving the planet. Corona was seventy light-years and many weeks away. She had assumed that her appointment orders meant that any Empyrion ship that picked her up would provide for her food and accommodations. Travel allowance? She'd never even heard of such a thing. If they tried to send her back—

She heard a sound and looked over her shoulder. The woman was back, accompanied by a muscular, middle-aged man. "A. F. Locke?"

She stood. "Yes."

"Come with me." She followed the man into the corridor. They were walking with their heads toward the center of the rotating station, the rotation itself providing the illusion of gravity. The man led her to a doorway, paused beside it, and looked at her with an uncomfortably hard stare. "Carlson Locke is dead?"

She nodded, her throat tight. "Cybots brought in what was left of his body. Particle bomb."

"One was stolen in a raid on the Fedder System a month ago," the man said. "Raiders."

"They just seemed to want food. They stole our crops."

"They may have been starving," the man said with no hint of sympathy. "Or they may want to sell it. Plenty of struggling colonies that would give top money. There seems to be a lot of this sort of theft going on lately. Earl Vodros and his allies have tightened restrictions—" He sighed and broke off, touching the wall. A door shimmered open. "I imagine you're too young to care about politics. Lucky you. You can have these quarters. I'm issuing you standard rations and giving you a limited clothing allowance. If I were you, I'd put together a basic wardrobe for your trip."

"Why are you helping me?" she asked him, surprised.

"Because I knew your father," the man said shortly, and he turned on his heel and walked away.

Life on the High Docks was dull but not difficult. There were pulsebooks to read, a gym for exercise, and people to talk to on the rare occasions when they were not working. There was even a commissary, a kind of small restaurant, where you could eat while watching the planet on the viewscreen, as if you were looking out a real window. Asteria practiced her boy act there.

The woman who had first interviewed her was named Celicia, Asteria learned, and she was a career administrator for the High Docks. "I haven't gone far in life," she said with a rueful smile one day as she and Asteria sat at a commissary table drinking jalava juice. "I was born right there on the planet.

You see that little cluster of lights on the equator, just inside the edge of the night?"

The planet far below was half in light, half in dark, and just inside the dark edge, near the equator, pinpricks of light marked out a city. "Central," Asteria said. "We visited it once."

"Big city," said Celicia mockingly. "Nearly a hundred thousand people."

"Were you born there?"

Celicia nodded. "My mother was an entertainment girl in the baron's court. I mean the old baron, not his son. Rumor had it that my father was one of his deputies. I never knew for sure. But I didn't want that kind of life, so I made sure to concentrate on studies that would lead me to a civil appointment. I didn't know it meant I'd wind up here." She looked musingly at Theron hanging in space.

Asteria asked, "Do you go back often?"

"Not since my mother died," Celicia replied. She thought for a minute. "I haven't left this station in six Standard years now. I don't intend to leave it. There's nothing for me down there."

"Me either," Asteria said.

"I'm off-duty now," Celicia said. "What are you doing?"

"I should be shopping," Asteria said. "Only I don't know what a cadet needs."

"They didn't send you a list?"

Asteria shook her head.

Celicia shrugged. "Well, the Academy will issue you a set of uniforms. You'll need clothes for travel and for downtime, though. I'd get three outfits if I were you. Tunics, pants, underwear, socks. You need space shoes, too, the soft-soled ones. You're wearing dirt boots. You need those only on the surface."

Asteria thanked her and did her shopping later that day, buying the three outfits and a synthetic tote bag to carry them in. Some toiletries completed her preparation. But she felt as if she were moving in a fog; nothing seemed real. Would the Academy buy her boy act? Should she even try to keep it up?

* * *

The High Docks could be a busy place when ships paused. And one seemed to dock about three or four times every Standard day. For a couple of hours, the commissary bustled, communicators twittered, and men and women hurried along the corridors. Then all became quiet until the next ship arrived.

Asteria made no attempt to speak to anyone, and she always remained in her tiny room—two and a half meters long, one and a half meters wide, with barely room for a bunk—when the daily shuttle from Sanctal arrived.

But the Bourse never came looking for her. On the fifth day of her stay aboard the station, while she was waiting out the daily shuttle visit, someone pinged her door. She dissolved it and saw the officer who had first given her the room. "Yes?"

He said gruffly, "Your ship for Corona's due tomorrow. The *Stinger,* an old-fashioned Defender-class destroyer. Don't expect much. Space Fleeters call her the *Stinker.* But she's heading for Corona, so I've booked you onto her."

"Thanks," Asteria said.

"Do you think you can get away with that disguise?" the man asked. "It's none of my business, but a candidate cadet shouldn't fool around like that."

"What do you mean?" Asteria asked, apprehensively.

"I mean I checked your orders," the officer said. "You're Andre F. Locke. Why are you pretending to be a girl?"

For a moment Asteria didn't know what to say. "W-well—you see, my—uncle was Carlson Locke—"

"I know who he was."

"He had a daughter," she said. "I sort of took her place. Because she had an appointment to the Academy."

"Really? Let me see your ID chip."

She unstrapped the transceiver and handed it over. The officer scanned it. "It says you're a boy, all right," he muttered. "But you think the Academy appointment's for your dead cousin? Is that it?"

Asteria nodded.

The officer handed her the transceiver again. He was staring hard at her. "Or is it the other way around?" he asked softly. "Are you really a girl?"

"My ID says—"

"I know about Carlson Locke," the man said. "I don't want to hear anything about you or your situation. But if you want this transceiver to identify you as a girl, I can arrange that."

"It's fine," she said.

"It's a simple thing to do. I'd do it for a nephew of Carlson Locke—or for his daughter."

Asteria's shoulders slumped. "Is it that obvious?"

The officer smiled. "My name's Altmon. Kris Altmon. I was a major in the Space Fleet until I retired. I came up the hard way, from the underclasses. Like Carlson Locke. You'll learn that most of the cadets at the Academy are Aristos. They look down on people like us. So we Commoners—we help each other out when we can. You'll have to learn to find people you can trust."

Asteria found herself heaving a sigh of relief. "Could you change the setting?"

"Give me the transceiver again." Altmon beckoned her, and she followed him to a maintenance bay. Half a dozen Cybots rested against the wall there, dormant. He tapped one of them, and its eyes lit up. "Unit S-939," Altmon said, "This ID chip has a faulty bit of data on it. Change the designation of gender from M to F."

"Yes, sir." The Cybot's delicate fingers dissected the transceiver, a hair-thin cable connected to the almost microscopic chip, and in a moment, everything had been reassembled. The Cybot returned the bracelet to Altmon, and he handed it over to Asteria.

"Don't depend on this too much," he warned her. "As I'm sure you know, the Academy admits both males and females, so there's no problem there. And the student body is so large that you just might hide in the throng. But there are other records that could be checked. Don't put your head up above the crowd at the Academy—don't make them eager to check out your background. You might just get by with it."

"Believe me, I'm not ungrateful or anything," Asteria said, strapping the wristlet back on. "But why are you helping me?"

"I told you. Because your uncle—or your father—was Carlson Locke," Altmon said. "Will you trust me enough to tell me which he was?"

"My father," she said. "I'm Asteria, his daughter."

"I think you can pretend to be a girl better if you really are one," Altmon said. "All right, your father, then. He's told you about the *Adastra,* hasn't he?"

"Just that he was on it."

Altmon snorted. "On it. Yes, he would say that. Come on, let's have a cup of cava."

They went to the commissary, where a few off-duty people sat at scattered tables. A couple of them rose hastily and left. "They're supposed to be on the job," Altmon said with a wink. "But High Docks isn't exactly a tight ship."

He brought the hot cups of cava to the table, and they sat sipping them. Then he said, "The *Adastra* dropped into normal space not expecting any trouble. There'd been no Tetra activity anywhere in the sector for nearly fifty years. It must have been a Tetra probe ship they encountered, though no one got a good look at it. The *Adastra*'s mission was to seed the second planet of the system with basic plant forms—algae, seaweeds, some bioengineered ferns that could stand the atmosphere and begin producing oxygen. In six thousand years, the planet might be made tolerable for lower forms of animal life, if the seeding took."

Asteria nodded, hanging on his every word. She'd never known any of this—never even guessed at it.

"They never got that far into the system," Altmon continued. "Something hit them, hard—the first attack wiped out the bridge, killing all the top-ranking officers. They were boarded by those spider warriors—you've seen pictures of them."

Asteria's throat closed. She had seen the photos of dead ones: horrors that were deceptively small, only a meter high, standing on six flexible, long legs, with four more appendages, shorter than the legs, serving as either arms or weapons, depending on how you looked at them. They were supremely deadly, incredibly fast, and well shielded against beam weapons. Only missiles could kill them.

"What happened?" she asked.

"About a third of the crew panicked and were abandoning ship. Your father was only a Chief Warrant Officer, but he organized resistance, scoured the command corridors, and killed the boarders, though he got hit with their heat beams. He was badly wounded, but he took control of the ship, dropped her into trans-space, and saved what was left of the *Adastra*—along with 804 lives. He was the acting captain on that strategic retreat."

Asteria shook her head, baffled. "I thought an ensign took command. That's what the histories say."

Altmon gave her a savage grin. "The Honorable Ensign Sanson Kalides *did* take command—a week later, back in Empyrion space. He came aboard at Six Stars Station and conned her back to dock at Corona. By then your father was in hospital bay. The ensign got official credit for saving the ship, an immediate promotion to lieutenant, and all the glory that a member of the Ruling Family would wish for. Your father got a set of cybernetic transplants and a grant of land for his services—and his promise never to speak about his true role in saving what was left of the crew. You see, Sanson Kalides was an ambitious politician back then. He wanted a swift promotion, and being the hero of the *Adastra* guaranteed that. Your father agreed because he was thinking of you—though you weren't even born then."

"He never said a word about that to me."

"He wouldn't have."

"How well did you know my father?" Asteria asked him.

Altmon took a last sip of his cava, set the cup down, and stood up. "We graduated in the same class. Two of my best friends were among the eight hundred aboard the *Adastra* who stuck with him. Kalides cracked down on the survivors. Warned them not to tell the true story to anyone. But you know how it is. Word gets around. And I liked your dad when we were in the Academy—even though he beat me in every test. And he was a good role model for me. Neither of us won an officer's commission. Commoners sometimes find the bar is set a little bit high for them." He smiled sourly and drank the last of his cava. His cup fumed and dissolved in the air.

* * *

The *Stinger* docked the next day for an eight-hour layover before resuming her trip to Corona. Asteria could tell she was an old ship, her hull patched in a hundred places, the plates showing microcraters from random impacts. She wasn't huge—the High Docks dwarfed her. A pulsebook had told her that the Defender-class destroyers typically carried a crew complement of one hundred, to a max of one hundred fifty. They were designed for fast maneuvering and were equipped with only a third of the firepower of more modern destroyers. These days, they were commanded by junior officers, often by senior lieutenants who were given the title "Captain" only as a courtesy.

Captain Rundell, then, was really Lieutenant First Class Rundell, a twenty-two-year-old man with a close-shaven head and no cheek tattoo. Without showing much interest, he scanned Asteria's admission letter, issued her a travel permit, and said, "We have one other cadet on this trip. I'll quarter you next to him. You'll have to take a warrant officer's berth, though— nothing luxurious. We're cramped."

"That will be fine," she said. "My father was a warrant officer."

"Keep out from underfoot," Rundell told her, "and we'll get along."

"Sir?" asked Asteria.

"What?"

"I was just wondering—you graduated from the Academy?"

"I certainly did. Now get along to your quarters. I have things to do." Asteria went. And she realized something: Lieutenant Rundell was an officer. And he was a Commoner like her. So it could be done.

If a Commoner could become an officer in the Fleet—a Commoner could fight the Raiders.

* * *

Asteria had been into space a few times before, into low orbit on planet-skimmers when her father had taken her to Central or to a short vacation on the Crystal Islands. She had never experienced interplanetary travel, though. Theron had no moon, and it was the only habitable planet in the system.

She knew not to expect much of the *Stinger*. It was a busy ship, with more than a hundred people aboard, pulling three watches. At any given time, a third of the crew members were operating the ship, and two thirds were either resting or off-duty. Still, the *Stinger* was small enough for even thirty-five people to make up a crowd.

Rundell gave her strict orders: She could visit the duty stations, but the bridge was off-limits unless he specifically invited her. She made the rounds, looking in on the engineering bay, where a dozen of the crew kept the ship's engines and systems running, a hive that smelled of ozone and that hummed with energy. Like all Fleet ships, the *Stinger* now had scattered weapons-control bays, each manned by a crew of five, one control officer and four gunners. With the officer's permission, the four bored crewmembers— skinny young men barely out of their teens—showed her the targeting and fire controls. Astronavigation was lonely; it was up to just the two of them to oversee the complex computations of space travel and of calculating a faster-than-light course.

The *Stinger*, she learned, was a ship of Commoners. It made sense; an Aristo would never be placed in a subordinate position to a Commoner officer. Lieutenant Rundell's position as captain meant that he would have no Aristocrats in his crew.

It could be done, she reminded herself again and again.

$$* * *$$

The day of the translight jump arrived. Asteria was curious about what faster-than-light drive would feel like. She had read that the effects of what everyone called FTL could be disturbing. Some people became comatose; others panicked. Once identified—and the only way to tell if you were likely to lose control was actually to experience the roll into trans-space and out again—those people who did have a problem with FTL had to be sedated for each translight jump.

She was the only newcomer aboard, so on Rundell's orders she reported to the sick bay for observation during the maneuver. A medical Cybot strapped her onto a gurney and said, "Try to relax."

As if she could. "How will I know when it starts?" she asked.

"You will feel it."

She waited. Nothing. And then—

She gasped. There was an incredible feeling of being *stretched*, as though her body had become pliable and was being elongated. A feeling of tightness, a blackness behind her eyes, a buzzing in her ears—

Then it was over. "Are we in trans-space?" she asked in a calm voice.

"Yes. Let me scan you."

The instruments twittered. "How am I?"

"Surprisingly well. I will release you. You have adapted to translight travel in a remarkably efficient manner."

"Thank you."

"The words 'Thank you' have no meaning to me."

Asteria swung off the gurney and opened the door of the sick bay. She turned into the corridor outside and immediately collided with a lanky redheaded boy about her age, slamming hard against him and staggering for balance. "Hey!" he growled in protest.

"I didn't see you," she said, recovering from the impact and frowning at him. "Anyway, *you* ran into *me*."

"You the cadet we picked up?" he asked. His red hair was short—not as short as hers—but still close-cropped. She could tell that if it grew out, it would be curly. His face looked pleasantly homely—big nose, green eyes, freckles, split with a jaunty grin.

She straightened her tunic and said coldly, "Yes, I'm on my way to the Academy."

He stuck out his hand, and she merely stared at it. Smiling broadly, he said, "Come on, meet a fellow victim. Dai Tamlin, a humble Commoner scholarship cadet."

42

"I'm Asteria," she said, still not taking his extended hand.

"What a name!" He smirked. "Better get a nickname before we reach Corona, or the Aristos will call you 'Hysteria.'"

She stared coldly at him, but her lips felt as if they might curl into a grin.

He dropped his hand, an uncertain expression flickering on his face. He darted an apprehensive look at her cheek, obviously searching for a tiny flame tattoo. "Uh—you're not an Aristocrat, are you? Because I didn't mean any class insult at all—"

"I'm no Aristo," she said shortly, pushing past him.

He hurried down the corridor after her. "Wait, wait. What did I say? I didn't mean anything by it! Hey, listen though, I was serious about a nickname. Don't call yourself Asteria. Shorten it to Aster or something, because those Aristos—"

"Don't run down Aristos to me," Asteria interrupted over her shoulder. "I've heard that at least they have manners." She reached her quarters, went inside, and solidified the door behind her. The lights came on in the compact room, and she threw herself onto her bunk.

A strange funk settled over her. She didn't know what kind of cadets she would meet at the Academy. She knew there would be other Commoners there. She only hoped some of them would be more appealing than Dai Tamlin.

Four

corona: The center of the Empyrion, the Corona is a closely packed cluster of eight star systems with a total of eleven habitable planets among them. One of these, Coriam, is exclusive to members of the Ruling Family and their servants and is off-limits to lesser Aristocrats and, of course, Commoners. Dromia, the second planet from its sun in the same system, became the operational capital of the Human Empyrion in E.Y.S. 1811 and is the site of the Royal Military Academy. A warm-temperate world, Dromia has 1.02 normal gravity, a day of 26.1 Standard hours duration, a year of 640 local days, divided into sixteen months of five eight-day weeks. Physical features include a permanent North Polar ice cap and a total of six continents, along with many—

Impatiently, Asteria skimmed through the dull parts of the pulsebook until she found the entry for the Academy.

The Royal Military Academy was founded as the Space Training Center in E.Y.S. 1802, fifty-one years after the translight breakthrough made deep space colonization and communication practical. Its original goal—to prepare crews for exploration, world-seeding, and the transportation of colonists to new worlds—was altered several times, first in E.Y.S 2001 after seven human-standard planets in the Varrian star *cluster, all within twenty light-years of Dromia, had been identified, researched, and cleared for colonization. In E.Y.S. 2209, the year that humans first encountered the savage Tetraploid race in the Vigan System, the name and mission of the institution was changed by royal decree. It became the Royal Military Academy and now had the task of training and equipping crews for fighting ships that would confront and deal with the alien menace—*

She scanned again. The images of the Academy came into her mind: it was located on a major island of Dromia, subtropical and lush with vegetation. The Academy had several subdivisions: Space Marines, Tech, Fleet Officer School, Surface Forces, Air Forces. Each one had a separate campus, each a sprawling complex of grounds and buildings. She was headed for Fleet Officer School, thanks to her cousin's legacy appointment. Hmm. A first-year student body of twelve thousand, approximately. Ninety percent of them were Aristos. Most Commoners went to either Tech, Space Marines, or Surface Forces. They made up the inventors and maintenance crews, the grunts who fought against the Raiders, the keepers of the Empyrion law on all the planets of the empire, the pilots who provided transportation.

Of course, Asteria thought, the Fleet didn't always fight against the Raiders. That seemed to happen only when the local ruling Aristo didn't think it was too much trouble to order retaliation. She pushed her resentment down and wondered what it would be like to be an officer.

Fleet Officers lived their lives in space.

Asteria felt a flutter of apprehension in the pit of her stomach. They had already reached the Dromia System and had dropped into normal space—another gut-wrenching sensation of being liquefied and distorted—and now were sailing in under normal ion thrust. The problem with trans-space was that in order to fold space-time into a kind of wave, dropping a ship into what amounted to a different universe—"think of it as surfing," a pulsebook had unhelpfully told her—the ship had to be well clear of space lanes and inhabited worlds. Theoretically, if a trans-space engine were engaged on the surface of a normal planet, one of two things might happen: the engine might simply explode, simultaneously evaporating several hundred thousand cubic kilometers of the planet's crust, or the engine might drop into trans-space and create a wormhole that would suck the planet to shreds within minutes.

Now here they were, so near that she could actually see the small blue marble of Dromia in the viewscreens, but still a few days away from docking and taking the shuttle down to the surface. She was in the last chapter of a short pulsebook, *The Entering Cadet's Guide to the Military Academy,* when Dai Tamlin's complaining voice interrupted her: "Wait, wait, wait. That's all we do."

Asteria bit back her irritation. Dai never greeted her or asked how she was. He simply started talking. And once he did, he was hard to stop. She didn't respond, and he went on, "New term doesn't begin until Dromia solstice, and that's more than a week after our landing date. I'm tired of waiting. I want to get busy."

Asteria said pointedly, "Some of us have tried studying," but the truth was that she, too, had grown tired of waiting. Her first thought back on Theron (when the infuriating elders had begun to size her up, as though she were a cut of meat to be handed out to the highest bidder) was simply to get away, and Andre's appointment seemed the easiest way.

But now—

"I suppose you're used to it. Waiting, I mean," Dai continued. "I've heard that Kamedes is timid even for a Fringe World governor."

"I wouldn't know," Asteria said. "I've never been offworld before."

"You said he didn't send help when Raiders attacked," Dai said.

"He didn't." Asteria frowned. "I think that he's afraid to call in Space Fleet to deal with bandits. That's a local issue. He'd look weak if he called in help. So he ignores them—as long as they don't try to attack his palace."

"And the religious people, the—what do you call them?"

"The Bourse," Asteria said. "They're no help either. They say the god of fate decides if a man will live or die. And my father and I were just Unbelievers to them, so they didn't really care about us."

Dai clapped her on the shoulder. "We'll care about us," he said cheerfully. "And when we graduate from the Academy and become Fleet pilots, we can chase those Raiders ourselves."

Asteria didn't reply, but she agreed. If no one else would do anything about the Raiders, she would go after them herself. Not now, of course. Not at thirteen. But in four years, she would graduate from the Academy as a pilot.

And when she was at the controls of a Space Fleet ship—

Well, there would be at least one Empyrean pilot who would go after the Raiders without a planetary administrator's command.

* * *

As she did every day, Asteria went that afternoon (by ship time; of course there was no real day or night, but all ships maintained the Standard twenty-five-hour day of Corona) to the gym.

There the gravity was tuned up to 1.05 normal to provide a more challenging workout. In a singlet and close-fitting exercise pants, Asteria spent forty minutes running on a treadmill, rested, and spent another forty working out on the weight sims. Or planned to. As she was about to try to break her bench press record, Dai Tamlin came wandering in again.

"Working out, I see," he said, sitting in the crunch chair—the one that stressed abdominal muscle exercises.

Asteria ignored him and drew in a deep breath.

"Fancy belt," he said. "What's it made of?"

Concentrate. Close your eyes. Find your center. Slowly now.

At first, the weight was like an immovable object, and then she managed to lift it. She felt the strain in her shoulders and biceps. She was pressing fifty Standard kilos—at 1.05 G, that worked out to 52.5. Her record had been forty-nine.

She felt as if she were lifting the weight of a world, but her straining arms began to straighten.

Dai jumped up. "Let me spot you," he said, moving around behind her head.

"No," she said between clenched teeth, and the effort of speaking distracted her. The weight teetered dangerously, and she began to have the panicky feeling that it would get away from her—

The belt around her waist sent a flash of—energy? It felt electric—into her skin, and suddenly the weight seemed halved.

She steadied the bar, lowered it, and raised it again, twice more. "What's the readout?" she asked.

"Fifty Standard," Dai said. "That's great for a girl! What do you weigh, about forty-five kilos?"

"Forty-seven point seven," she said, wondering where the burst of strength had come from. She felt a raging thirst. "And I think a girl can do anything a boy can do."

"I didn't mean—"

She interrupted irritably, "Switch off the sim."

Dai did, and the bar suddenly weighed almost nothing. Asteria got up and went to the water dispenser, taking a long, long, cool drink. Dai sat back down on the crunch machine, shaking his head. "You pressed more than your own weight," he said. "One thing's for sure, you'll pass the Academy PT entrance exam. That just calls for a guy pressing 95 percent and a girl pressing 75 percent—"

"They should be the same," Asteria said impatiently.

"Maybe. Uh, where'd you get the belt?" asked Dai.

"From my father," Asteria said, and it wasn't untrue.

"It's not standard issue. They'll make you give it up at the Academy."

"I don't mind." *If they can figure some way to take it off me. Nothing I've tried works.*

"My weak spot's going to be unarmed combat," Dai said. "I've practiced, but I'm not very good. How about you?"

Asteria felt a little throb of sorrow. She and Andre, wasting their time with the Okida moves. "I'll just try my best," she said.

"Want to practice a little? I know Jai-chon, Okida, and a little Mazzetta."

"I only know a bit of Okida."

"Let's do a round or two then. I'll go easy on you."

"Oh, will you promise?" she asked sarcastically.

"Sure. I'll pull the moves. We'll just work on speed."

"Well," she said, trying to sound undecided. "If you won't really hurt me."

The adjacent room was set up with a padded floor and walls. Dai insisted on binding his forehead and on tying a red ribbon around his left biceps, the mark of the formal student. Asteria said, "I've never been to an Okida master, so I don't have the sigils."

"That's all right," he said. "They're not really needed, but I sort of feel they help me."

They faced each other and bowed formally, part of the ritual. They fought barefoot and open-handed. As they circled each other tensely, each looking for an opening, Asteria reminded herself of the tenets of combat: *Respect your opponent. Divert force into harmlessness. Use an opponent's thrust against the opponent. Be quick.*

Dai lunged in, feinted to the left, and then tried to catch Asteria's wrist for a throw, but she snaked away, skipping to the side. He blinked in surprise. "Nice move."

"Thanks."

They danced around each other. Dai was more wary now, keeping his chin down, his green eyes sharp. He seemed in no hurry.

Patience wins more battles than strength, Asteria reminded herself.

"Aren't you going to do anything?" Dai asked at length.

"We'll see."

Without warning, Dai dropped to one arm and swept his legs

around, trying to trip her. Asteria skipped over them and leaped back before he could counterswing, and then as he sprang to his feet, she did a forward roll, catching his legs and shoving hard. Dai tumbled sprawling on his face, and she moved in for two quick ear slaps, then out again, and into defensive posture.

"That could have hurt!" Dai complained, regaining his feet.

"I pulled them," Asteria said in a tone of innocence. And without giving any hint, she did the Snake Strike, thrusting in low and hard to seize his leg—but he leaped, higher than she had thought possible, and she tucked, rolled, and spun back onto her feet as he moved forward and tapped the inside of her left elbow before retreating.

"I could have broken it if I'd wanted," he said.

"And I could have knocked you out when I got your ears," growled Asteria.

Anger is your enemy.

She breathed deeply. He lunged at her. She reached for a throw-hold, missed, and his momentum spun her to the mat. Before she could recover, he had seized her wrist and held it firmly behind the small of her back. "My fall," he said.

"I—don't—concede!"

Again she felt a strange, electric sensation from the belt around her waist. And then—

Later, Asteria couldn't even remember how she had done it, but she twirled her whole body, lay on her back and shoulders, and kicked Dai in the stomach, hard. He lost his grip, tumbled backward, and a second later, she had a knee on his solar plexus and two fingers on his carotids. She refrained from pressing and knocking him out.

"I yield," he gasped.

She rose, wondering why it was so hard to do so—she'd felt an impulse to render her foe unconscious. Worse. She'd felt like ripping his head off!

Dai shook his head. "How did you do that? I've never seen that kind of move, and I've been taking lessons for five years!"

"I come from a Fringe World," she told him. "Out there, we have to make our own fun."

She walked out of the combat room, aware of his astonished gaze following her. *Serves him right*, she thought. *Maybe it will keep him from bothering me. Or at least maybe it will make him more interested in me.* She wasn't quite sure which she preferred.

* * *

The *Stinger* docked at an enormous synchronous station—the size of a small moon. Dai and Asteria shouldered their bags and found their way to the Academy shuttle, a small craft with room for a dozen. The pilot was a Cybot.

"Are we the only passengers?" Dai asked it.

"You are the only two on schedule today," the pilot replied. "It is early. Orientation will not begin for another Standard week."

"Then take us down," Dai told it.

Asteria sat staring out the window. The station receded; the shuttle rolled—not too uncomfortably, because as a small ship, it had no artificial gravity, and they were in free fall weightlessness—and then turned its nose toward Dromia. Its oceans were a brilliant turquoise, its white cloud patterns elaborate etchings.

"Scared?" Dai asked.

"Not particularly," Asteria said.

"Oh." Dai drummed his fingers on the arm of his seat. "I am," he admitted.

"Why?" she asked.

He shrugged. "I'm the first member of my family to make it to the Academy. I won the planetary competition this year on Hovia—do you know Hovia?"

"I've heard of it." Asteria remembered what little she knew: Hovia was a mining world, harvesting a rich asteroid belt. It was a Middle World, not close to the center of the Empyrion, but not far enough out to be on the Fringe. Like many other Middle Worlds, it was said to be moderately prosperous and moderately restless under Empyrean rule.

"We get to send one candidate a year to the Academy," Dai said. "One! And our population is three times your world's."

"I don't know how many Theron sends," Asteria replied. "Anyway, I'm a legacy. I didn't compete for your scholarship."

"If a scholarship student washes out, he can't go home again," Dai muttered. "It's a humiliation to his whole family."

"Would your family treat you like a failure?" she asked.

He shrugged. "My dad supervises the wolframite industry. He started as a miner and worked his way up. He ought to be made the administrator for the industry, but there's a minor Aristo in that position. Lower-level Aristos run everything. Dad can't go any further himself, so he's hoping I'll get into the Fleet, where even a Commoner can be promoted all the way to the top."

"In theory," Asteria said.

"Yeah, in theory. Dad's always called me brainy but lazy. When I was boarding the shuttle to take me offworld, he didn't say good-bye. He just said, 'Come back a graduate or don't come back at all.'"

"And he wants you to be a pilot."

"No, he'd be happy if I went in as a second lieutenant in surface security forces. He just wants me to graduate, that's all." Dai shrugged. "I want to be a pilot. I think my family's hugged the ground for too many years already."

"You'll make it."

"Sure," he said with a sudden grin. "I can do anything!" Then he looked away and nervously added, "Provided I don't wash out."

"Come on. You'll make it through."

"Yeah," Dai said. He took a deep breath. "But I've never been around Aristos much. You can't upset them or treat them with disrespect. And I'm not sure I believe they're born better than we are. If you get in trouble with an Aristo at the Academy, they can wash you out, I hear. So I guess I worry a lot."

Asteria looked at him with mingled irritation and amusement. "You know there's an easy cure for your worries, don't you?"

He glanced at her in surprise. "There is? I wish you'd tell me."

"Don't wash out," she said and turned back to the window. Dromia had swelled to planet size. A moment later, the shuttle bounced turbulently—they had entered the atmosphere.

Somewhere below them the whole future waited.

part 2
the god of 2.5

FIVE

Asteria sat fidgeting. Next to her, Dai occupied a chair, but he wasn't exactly sitting—not comfortably, anyway, but stiffly, his back straight, his chin tucked in, staring straight ahead. He looked terrified. Their half hour on the planet had not calmed his worries.

The anteroom was in one of the older buildings on campus. The Academy was the size of a city, with all the architectural variety of a settlement more than three thousand years old. The administration building stood twelve stories tall and was made of old-fashioned red brick, with arched, leaded windows and a floor tiled with some hard tan-colored stone that showed fossils, shells, and small skeletons of fish-like creatures. Old-fashioned electric lights still hung suspended on chains like displays in a museum. They were obviously not used, because the ceilings glowed with the standard tribiolumes.

The chairs seemed new, though they must have been designed for maximum discomfort. Asteria hoped she didn't look as squirmy as Dai did to her.

The midclassman who had shown them to the anteroom reappeared in the sharply arched doorway. "Come on, serfs," he said with a mocking grin. "The dragon lady is ready for you."

Serfs. All freshmen were called that—because they "belonged" to the upperclassmen, who had the right to treat them like servants. They followed their guide through the inner doorway. A woman with hair the color of steel, wearing the dark blue uniform of a vice admiral in the Star Fleet space division, stood at a window, her hands behind her back. "Thank you, Scanlen," she said. "That will be all."

"Aye," said the midclassman, saluting. He took one step back, did a crisp about-face, and walked out of the office.

"Entering Cadets Tamlin and Locke," the woman said, turning and staring at them. "The first thing you have to learn is to come to attention when a senior officer is present."

Dai somehow managed to stiffen even more, and Asteria put her shoulders back and stood tall. The woman came and circled them, gazing at them critically. Asteria saw with surprise that she had a small scar on her left cheek—as though a tattoo of the minor Aristocracy had been removed. The vice admiral stood in front of her and said, "Probationary Cadet Locke, ask your friend to show you the proper stance before you meet another officer. At ease, you two."

Asteria relaxed. Next to her, Dai sagged perhaps a millimeter.

"I am Vice Admiral Chen," the woman said. "Commandant of Cadets. Let us hope that in the coming months you won't see very much of me—because if you do, that means you are in serious trouble. You've arrived very early, but that may be to your advantage. You have a few days to familiarize yourselves with deportment and procedures. You'll be quartered in Bronze Barracks 1. There's a female wing and a male wing. Make sure you're in the right one, and don't trust the upperclassmen to tell you which is which. You should be able to tell from the latrines. You will be issued uniforms; you will wear them at all times when you are awake and active on the campus. You may not leave campus until midterm, and then only if you are maintaining an average of 2.5 in your studies. After midterm, if your grades are acceptable and you have no demerits to work off, you may have one half day a month leave time in Haven. Any questions?"

Neither Dai nor Asteria responded.

"Then get to your quarters and collect your gear. Memorize the student code pulsebook. Dismissed."

Dai came to attention, saluted, and stepped back before pivoting, and Asteria tried to imitate him. Vice Admiral Chen's voice stopped her at the door: "Probationary Cadet Locke, remain."

She froze in her tracks. As Dai marched out the door, she turned, wondering what she had done. She thought back to the guidebook: Should she come to attention? Better to do so than risk a demerit.

"At ease," the vice admiral said. She nodded toward another uncomfortable-looking chair. "Sit."

Asteria did, and when the vice admiral stared at her, Asteria matched her icy blue gaze. Silence stretched out.

Finally, the admiral broke it. "You are the nephew of Carlson Locke," she said in a strangely teasing tone.

"No, Commandant. The daughter," Asteria said in a level voice. "My cousin was Andre Locke. I'm...Aster."

"Indeed. Then our records must be in some disorder."

The vice admiral again let the silence go on. She looked as if she expected some kind of response.

"My cousin Andre is dead," Asteria said. "So is my father."

The vice admiral did not change her expression. "I see. How did they die?"

Asteria swallowed the lump in her throat, and quickly, directly, she told the vice admiral about the raid.

The woman drew in a deep breath. "There have been no requests for aid from the administration of Theron," she said. "No reports of an attack."

"No, Commandant," Asteria said. "The Bourse of Sanctal can't ask for help on their own, and the planetary government thinks it's merely a local problem."

"That would be Kamedes?"

"Yes, Commandant."

"I see. So you have decided to take your cousin's place at the Academy."

"It was that or be forced to marry into the Bourse," Asteria said. "If the Academy won't have me—"

"A legacy appointment is due to any child, niece, or nephew of Carlson Locke," the vice admiral said. "You didn't know that?"

"No, Commandant."

"You know that your father was something of a hero?"

"I know he was badly wounded."

"Do you know the whole story?"

Asteria thought for a moment. "I—I'm not sure."

"You probably don't. But Space Fleet owed your father a great deal after the *Adastra* incident. Yes, he was wounded, but his efforts helped the acting captain return the ship safely to our space. I see by our records that you're an orphan now. Your mother has been dead for some years." Without waiting for a response, the vice admiral reached for her cap and said, "Come with me. Let's walk around the campus."

The day was warm, nearly uncomfortably warm to someone

raised on the chilly Uplands of Theron. Outside the administration building, Vice Admiral Chen said, "You should walk to my left, half a step behind me. Speak only when I give you permission. Come."

The campus of the space division of the Royal Military Academy had a kind of military beauty to it, everything severely landscaped, symmetrical. The lawn was a vivid shade of turquoise. Flower beds lined the walkways, the plants in them standing in ranks like a colorful army.

Away from the Administration section, the architecture became more uniform. The classroom buildings, scattered enough to make the grounds seem airy and open, tended to be collections of long, low wings with arched roofs, like cylinders half-buried in the ground. The vice admiral pointed some out: The Space Sciences building. Biology. Chemistry. History and Government. They came at last to a plaza shaded by umbrella-like trees with drooping spear tip–shaped lavender leaves.

Asteria had seen impressions of the campus before, in pulsebooks, but the real thing seemed different from what she had expected. For one thing, there were few people about. She had expected to lose herself in a crowd, but now, alone with the vice admiral, she felt uneasy, exposed, a moving target. A fountain jetted in the center of the paved opening between the trees; benches, arranged again in severe symmetry, surrounded the central fountain. Beyond the fountain stood a golden statue, somewhat larger than life-sized, of two men.

"Read the plaque," the vice admiral said, nodding toward the base.

But first Asteria stared at the two men. A heroic figure, all chiseled features and determination, supported a clearly wounded young man. The younger man's features seemed vaguely familiar. Asteria looked down at the inscribed plaque and read:

THE HONORABLE ENSIGN SANSON KALIDES
HERO

"That's supposed to be my father he's supporting," Asteria said dryly.

"Sanson Kalides—Lord Kalides now—saved the *Adastra* and brought her safely into port with the surviving crew aboard," said the vice admiral. In a quieter tone, she added, "Despite the fact that he wasn't actually aboard the ship at the time of the Tetra attack. The ship's captain, Princeps Makath Kyseros, is revered as the officer who gave his life to allow the ship to escape from the attackers. A Commoner Chief Warrant Officer is remembered as someone who was badly wounded and whose life was saved by Lord Kalides, and that is all. That is the official version. It is very important to the prestige of the Kyseros family that these are the accepted facts. You understand?"

"Yes, Commandant."

"Do you? I would advise you not to discuss your family with anyone here. Most of the cadets around you will be Aristocrats," the vice admiral warned. "Be aware of that. Be careful about what you say. Watch your temper. Do you have an advocate on Theron to watch over your affairs?"

Absently, Asteria shook her head, but then remembered her place as a lowly candidate cadet. "No, Commandant. The Bourse are looking after the farm. I'm supposed to inherit it, but I don't know—"

"It's a matter of Empyrean law," the vice admiral said. "Too important to you to allow the Bourse to take care of your interest without someone supervising them. I'll have an advocate appointed. Kamedes will listen to me. Dismissed, Cadet. The Bronze Barracks are that way, beyond the Language and Communications building. On the double."

Asteria saluted, the unsmiling Vice Admiral Chen returned the salute, and then the new cadet did an about-face—not as clean as Dai's had been—and trotted away, feeling uncertain. She wondered if the library was open yet. She had a lot to learn about Empyrean law, about the Academy, about…well, everything.

* * *

One advantage of having turned up early for the term was that Asteria had her choice of rooms. Barracks at the Academy were like dormitories—at least the cadets did not all sleep in one vast bedroom. Still, their quarters seemed made to accustom them to the cramped living areas on starships. Asteria's compartment—she chose it because it was nearest one of the outside doors—was no larger than the little cubby that she had occupied on the flight to Corona. The bunk swung down from the wall. When it was in the upright position, she had access to two wide drawers beneath it, which held everything she owned: civilian clothing, pulsebook reader, textbooks.

She had so few possessions that half of one drawer gave more than enough room. At the foot of the bunk, a recess served as a closet. She hung the five gray first-year uniforms there, along with her gym clothing. A shelf above the hangers held her boots, dress shoes, and athletic shoes. With the bed folded up, she could sit in a chair that folded out from one wall and open up a desk that folded from the adjoining wall: there was her computer and AI unit.

Very stark. She had a few pangs of claustrophobia, but she thought she could get used to it. Hoped she could. If she got antsy in her tiny room, she had lots of space to roam—at least until the other cadets arrived and settled in. The Bronze Barracks were huge, tawny cubical structures made of the same fossil-bearing stone that paved the floors in the Admin Building. The first-year mess hall was on the north side of the small park in the center of a cluster of the four Bronze Barracks. Because it was summer break, the mess hall was operating on a very reduced scale. Meals were at set times, and she had to eat fast. The food was fairly tasteless, and that was the best compliment Asteria could give it.

"I'm taking your advice," she told Dai as they finished their first meal on campus. "I'm going to tell everyone my name is Aster."

"Good idea," Dai said. He looked around the mess hall. Its long tables could accommodate a thousand cadets. "It seems weird to be here all by ourselves."

Asteria nodded. "Lucky for us, though. We'll have time to memorize the student code."

"I've done that already. I can boil it down to a few principles: Do what you're told. Don't attract attention. Don't be different. Always let the Aristos win."

"Same as at home, then."

Dai gave her a long stare. "You didn't have much to do with Aristos where you came from, did you?"

She shook her head. "I didn't have much to do with anybody. I was raised on a farm. No neighbors. My dad and my cousin were almost the only people I saw."

"You never went into civilization?"

"Our farm was civilized!" she snapped. "Yes, I went into Sanctal—that was the nearest town—with Dad or Andre a few times a month. Sometimes we went as far as Central, where the government center is. You know, dealing with pensions and taxes and stuff."

"My planet was thick with Aristos," Dai said moodily as they finished eating. On the table in front of them, their plates were quietly dissolving, taking the last scraps of food along with them as they vaporized into curling white mist that quickly dissipated. "Inspectors, auditors, advisors, administrators." Dai lowered his voice: "All of them idiots. You get a lower-level Aristo too dumb or lazy to make it in the Academy or the Royal Colleges, they get appointed to positions like that. The safety advisor for our mines was a baronet. Advisor! He'd come by once a year and say, 'Continue your safety procedures,' and collect ten percent of our profits!"

"We didn't have inspectors on Theron. Too far out, I guess."

"Lucky."

They walked back to Bronze 1, but before they reached the entrance, both of their wrist communicators chirped.

"Yes?" they answered simultaneously.

The same artificial voice came from both communicators: "You are to report to Central Medical for your physical at 1350. That is twenty-three minutes from now."

"Physical," said Asteria. Her eyes flashed to her belt.

Dai glanced at her. "You sound worried. You sick?"

"Not exactly," she replied.

* * *

An hour later, wearing just her underwear, Asteria perched on the edge of an examination table as the medical Cybot brought in a human doctor, a Vallerian woman with the peculiar greenish complexion of her people. "You'll have to remove the belt," she said.

"I can't," Asteria told her.

Frowning, the doctor touched the metallic belt—and yelped. She shook her hand. "Did you feel that?" she asked sharply.

"No," Asteria said. "The same thing happened when the Cybot touched it."

The Cybot said mildly, "It delivered an electrical charge of more than five thousand volts. Fortunately, the amperage was—"

"Not high enough to cause damage, just discomfort," the doctor interrupted. "That's not Empyrean technology."

"I don't know what it is," Asteria confessed. "It belonged to my father."

"Doesn't it have a release?"

"No." Asteria tugged at it, showing the doctor how the plates had interlocked. "If I try to push it off, it tightens," she said.

"We can cut it off—"

"Negative," the Cybot said. "The material is at least fifteen times more resistant than synsteel, and the circuitry performs in ways I cannot analyze. Attempting to destroy or cut it is too dangerous."

"You're not supposed to wear anything like that," the doctor grumbled.

"I can't help it!"

"Wait here."

Asteria wrapped her arms around herself—the room felt chilly—and waited for a long half hour. Then the door opened again, and Vice Admiral Chen came in together with the green-skinned doctor. "At ease," she said as Asteria hopped off the examination table and brought herself to attention. "Causing trouble already, Cadet Locke?"

"No, Commandant. At least—I'm not trying to, Commandant!"

"Leave us," Chen said to the doctor. She glanced at the Cybot. "You too."

As soon as they were alone, the vice admiral said, "Tell me about that thing. The truth, please."

Asteria told her how she had found the belt, how she had tried it on, and how it had apparently decided not to leave her.

Chen nodded. "It may be alien tech," she said. "In the fighting aboard the *Adastra,* several of the Tetra spiders were disabled and later examined. I've never heard of anything like this—but of course Empyrean policy is not to copy alien tech. Perhaps your father kept this as a souvenir."

"I don't know about that."

For some moments, Chen stood in thought. Then she opened the door and called the doctor and the Cybot back in. "Rate this as a third-class medical device," she said to the doctor. "Those are permitted."

"But—"

"I'll take responsibility," Chen said. "As you were."

"Aye, Admiral."

Once the doctor was alone with Asteria, she shook her head. "I hope we won't get into trouble for this. Cybot, record the belt as a third-class medical device to—oh, say to aid posture."

The rest of the examination proved nothing except that Asteria was in excellent health. Finally, she was permitted to dress. Next came the records work: forms to complete, surveys to fill out, and even some requests to make. She had "no preference" for permanent barracks assignment, "none" for next of kin, and "remain on campus" for the between-terms leave periods. Finally, with no hesitation at all, she checked that she would "accept" the offer of a third-term experience in space, if her grades permitted. She logged her forms in and was sent back to her barracks—on the double.

She jogged across the campus, feeling a little disoriented. Dromia spun a little more slowly on its axis than Theron, and its day came to about 26.1 Standard hours, as opposed to 23.4 on her homeworld. She had the feeling that the sun should be lower in the sky.

The days at the Academy were going to be very long.

SIX

Of the 125 girls in Bronze 1, 102 were Aristos. In a way, this didn't matter. To upperclassmen, all first-term Midshipmen, whether Aristo or Common, were serfs to be ordered around, belittled, and ridiculed. And they were supposed to take it. Silently.

Asteria felt like an outsider among all those Aristos, but even so, it wasn't as bad as she had feared. She could almost hide in the crowd, because the school had nearly equal numbers of boys and girls. At least the other girls in her barracks didn't hang an annoying nickname on her. They called her "Aster," which she now claimed as her name.

That was a relief, because to all the upperclass students who bothered to notice her at all, she was "Disaster." Dai hadn't thought of that variant when he had suggested that she shorten her name. Nor had he thought it necessary to change his own name—so to all the upperclass students who pushed him around, he was now "Die, Scum!"

Lots of fun.

"Serf!" an upperclassman might call to her suddenly. "How many rules do you have to obey?"

"Twelve hundred and twenty-one!" she had to respond immediately.

With an evil grin, the questioner might then demand, "And what is Rule 1013, subclause A?"

If Asteria were slow in reciting it—"An off-duty cadet must always maintain an active personal communicator in case of emergency transmissions"—then the upperclassman might give her a demerit, order her to perform some personal service like cleaning his or her boots, or command her to drop and execute twenty-five push-ups. But she could handle it. She could handle anything. She had to—for her father, for what she had lost. All she had to do was think of the charred cinders and smoky rubble the Raiders had left of her farm.

Beginning on the first day of classes, Asteria had to get up early, 0500 hours. She and the other girls in her dorm crowded into the showers, hastily soaped up and rinsed, and then dried and dressed. By 0545, they had to be in formation outside the barracks and jog to the dining hall. On the double.

"Everything is on the double," grunted black-haired Bala Takeen, one of her dorm mates, the first day. The upperclassman conducting them heard the remark and issued Bala a demerit for talking in ranks.

They were also supposed to maintain silence at the table. They almost had to, because the schedule gave them only twenty minutes to eat. Then they jogged again to physical training class, which began around the time the sun rose at 0615.

"Hi," Dai said to her on their first day in the gym complex. "I'm glad we have some classes together."

Asteria nodded.

Dai smiled. "We can talk here," he said. "As long as we're silent when the proctors—"

"Class, attention!" said the Cybot. Two hundred and fifty students stood stiffly. The Cybot said, "You will report here for physical training six days a week. Three days a week will be spent in zero-gravity training, alternating with three days in normal or enhanced-gravity training. You are going to be split into ten classes of twenty-five students each. As I call your names, assemble here and then follow your instructor. The Honorable Orlin Avers. Viscount Laslik Azora. Deria Basila—"

Dai wound up in the same training class as Asteria. Two of the classes followed an instructor to a gym in which the walls, floor, and ceiling were all padded. "Zero G," murmured Dai.

Sure enough, their instructor, a woman lieutenant named Tasenos, told them, "This is Zero-Gravity Facility Five. You will report here every other day. Today, we have orientation. Form up into five rows of ten. Dress left and right."

Asteria had never heard the term, but Dai was in the row right ahead of her, and she saw him stretch both arms out to his side. She did the same, and the cadets shuffled until they stood at double arm's length from each other. The instructor nodded, stepped back, and said, "Going to zero gravity now."

Gravigenerators whined. Asteria realized they were in the walls and ceiling—gravity actually was not being canceled out, but equalized, so that the walls and ceiling tugged on her just as strongly as the floor. She felt a momentary sensation of falling.

"Kick off from the floor," the instructor said. "Gently."

Asteria tapped her toe and felt herself rising into the air. Ahead of her, Dai kicked too hard. He soared five meters up and bounced off the ceiling, tumbling back down. A number of others had done the same thing.

"You will have to learn control," the instructor said sternly. "Good job, Allmon, Chresler, Locke, Thursby. Microgravity of point one."

The gentle gravity brought them all back to the floor. "We are going to do that again," the instructor said. "And we'll repeat it until you can rise in formation. If you don't want to be bored, catch on quickly."

The second time, Asteria was a little too timid with her tap, and the instructor said, "Locke, do it the same way you did the first time. Tamlin, you're still trying to jump into orbit. Take it down by half. Microgravity of point one. Do it again…"

At the end of the period, Dai said, "I think I've got it now."

"I don't like zero G," Asteria muttered. "It makes me feel clumsy. How do you judge mass and trajectory?"

"You'll learn," Dai assured her. They had to form up and jog off again to their next class—on the double.

The routine repeated the next day, except this time they reported for normal-gravity physical training in another wing of the gym complex. The instructor, a warrant officer who was about twenty-five and who looked as though he had been designed by powerbots, teamed the twenty-five yellow-clad cadets up to see what they knew of self-defense. Asteria had sort of hoped to be paired with Dai, because it would be fun to shove him around a little, but instead she found herself facing a rangy young man with a challenging, superior smile: the nametape on his yellow jumpsuit identified him as Kayser, K (MASTRAL, CT).

The instructor called him "my lord." Three Aristos who seemed to be friends of his called him "Mastral." Properly speaking, Asteria should have referred to him as "my lord" or

"Your Lordship." Looking at his arrogant expression, however, she decided she didn't like him enough to call him anything, and so she chose to avoid the problem by not speaking to him.

"My lord," said the warrant officer, "you shall be the attacker. Locke, defend against him."

The Aristo grinned savagely as the two of them stepped inside the thirty-meter diameter combat ring etched on the gym floor. "How much shall I hurt her?"

"Don't try for anything disabling, my lord," the warrant officer told him in a toneless, matter-of-fact way. He stepped back and pointed Asteria into the left zone of the combat circle, Kayser into the right. He raised his hand. "Remain within the boundary. Anyone forced out of the circle loses automatically. Ready? At my signal. Very good, take your positions…go!" He slashed his hand down, starting the sparring round.

Kayser pressed forward, arms raised as he invaded Asteria's half of the circle. Asteria saw that he was using bladehand, a flashy but not efficient style of fighting art. Andre had taught her a little of it, but he had said dismissively, "Aristo boys use it to impress girls who don't know anything about fighting." Asteria wondered how much Kayser knew. He certainly looked confident as he moved toward her, semi-crouching, his hands flashing, his eyes mocking.

Asteria circled carefully to the left, keeping her gaze on Kayser's midsection—the abdomen, she had learned from her cousin, was the key to judging an opponent's movement. Eyes could deceive, and legs could feint, but the midsection always told the true story. When she saw Kayser's muscles tense, she readied herself. He waded in, thrusting and slashing with his flattened hands, trying to strike a nerve nexus or open her guard and let him deliver a decisive blow that would knock her out of the circle.

He probably expected her to backpedal, but instead Asteria stepped forward and met him with Mantis hands, her forearms interrupting his blows, warding them off harmlessly to the side. She saw the look of surprise in his eyes—just before she clipped his chin with the heel of her right hand, snapping his head back and making him stagger. His friends shouted and objected: "Foul!"

Kayser glared at her, shaking his head, opening and closing his mouth.

The warrant office coughed in a sort of mild warning. "It is not considered good form for a Commoner to touch an Aristocrat's face, Locke. Even in sparring practice."

"Sorry," she said without looking at the muscular instructor. "I'll hit him lower from now on."

"Think so, Disaster?" growled Kayser. He stepped forward, more wary now, with his hands flexing before they assumed the bladehand flatness. He was slower and more deliberate this time, feinting in, trying to judge her reactions. And then, with no visible warning, he swung his leg around in a hard abdominal kick.

She twisted away from it, causing him to miss, caught his foot, and spun him, and when his back was to her, she delivered her own kick to the small of his back. He fell forward flailing and stumbling, but he was too far off-balance to prevent himself from staggering across the perimeter of the ten-meter circle.

"Out!" shouted the warrant officer.

"Doesn't count!" snapped Kayser, spinning around to face her again. "She kicked me from behind!"

"That is permitted, my lord," the officer said coldly.

"Not this time." Kayser stepped back into the circle, his face glowing with anger. "I have to teach this little Commoner Disaster a lesson."

"It's all right," Asteria said. "I'll fight him again. Best two out of three rounds."

"Stay in control, my lord," warned the warrant officer. "I'll count any more unfounded protests against you."

Kayser waded in again, so worked up, so shot with adrenaline, that Asteria couldn't block every thrust. She caught a hard, stinging one just off-center of her solar plexus, and another one made her ears ring. It was not forbidden, it seemed, for an Aristo to slam a Commoner on the chin.

But Kayser was clearly not used to a high-gravity world, even one as marginally higher as Dromia (1.02 G) was to Coriam (1.0 G—supposedly the same mass and gravity as the long-lost homeworld of humanity, Earth). His attacks had lost some of their edge, and his movements slowed. Asteria, by contrast, felt remarkably fresh. In fact, she had the momentary illusion that Kayser was moving in slow motion. She watched for her opening.

Trying to lure him forward, she pretended to be staggered by a blow to her shoulder and backed to the edge of the circle. If she read him right, he would rush her, trying to push her outside the boundary—

With a wicked grin on his face, Kayser suddenly snarled, "Grab her!"

With her attention focused on Kayser, Asteria was not guarding her back. Two of Kayser's friends leaped into the circle, grabbed her arms, locking her elbows, holding her still, a stationary target. The warrant officer blasted his whistle to signal a foul, but the Aristos ignored him. "Hah!" Kayser leaped forward, his arm drawn back for a sharp blow—

From the metal belt beneath her tunic, a wave of strength shot into Asteria. She wrenched her arms down, breaking the boys' hold on her, then swung her hands up, stunning both of the young Aristos—and it had happened so fast that Kayser still had not connected. With a strange detachment, as though she had stepped out of her own body, Asteria pivoted to her left, seized Kayser's thrusting wrist with both of her hands, and pulled as he put all his force into the useless blow. A second later, he lay sprawled on the floor, outside the circle, facedown and momentarily silent.

"My lord," the warrant officer said, lowering his whistle, "this is the second time your opponent forced you from the ring. You lose."

Shaking his head, his face scarlet with fury, Kayser pushed himself to his knees and then rose to his feet. He turned on his two friends, turning his anger on them. "Stupid! You were supposed to help me!" He spun around and strode off toward the men's showers.

"My lord," the instructor called after him, "class is not over."

"It is for me," Kayser shot back, not bothering to look around. The two boys who had grabbed Asteria—their name tapes identified them as Broyden and Gull—writhed in an agony of indecision, taking a step as though to follow their retreating leader but then losing their nerve and remaining with the class, their heads down, not meeting anyone's gaze.

His face devoid of expression, the instructor said, "Take a demerit each, Broyden, Gull. Tell Lord Mastral that he is to take one demerit for leaving class early. The rest of you, note that Locke did not raise a protest, as she was permitted to do. I like that kind of initiative. As for you, probationary Cadet Locke, you have good speed, but you must learn to anticipate your enemy's moves. In actual combat, being fully aware of what is happening behind you as well as in front of you might make the difference between life and death. Remember that."

Asteria nodded, feeling like herself again. "I'll remember it."

"Good. Broyden, team with Vanslav. Vanslav, you will be the attacker. In the ring, both of you. At my signal. Ready—"

A few minutes after that bout—which ended in an inconclusive draw between the two Aristos—the class ended, and the cadets hurried off to the showers. On the way, Valesa Storm, a Commoner girl said very quietly to Asteria, "Good for you. But you made Lord Mastral look foolish."

Bren Maddon, another Commoner from Asteria's barracks, nudged Valesa. "Shh. Not so loud." But she also whispered to Asteria, "You should watch your back from now on."

"Thanks." After they had showered, the girls had to split up, heading for different classes.

Kayser and his two friends were waiting as they left the gym. Kayser said, "Brought a bodyguard, Disaster?"

"Just like you did," Asteria said. "Want to practice some bladehand?"

Gull and Broyden took a step back, Gull murmuring, "Mastral, it's a court-martial offense to fight."

"We're going to be late to class," Broyden whined.

With his face flaming, Kayser said, "Who said anything about fighting? Why don't you go out for the War Games, Disaster? That's where breeding tells. Meet me in the games if you think you won't be humiliated. Let's go!"

He and his two friends jogged away. Asteria felt someone touch her shoulder reassuringly, and Bren said, "Good luck, Aster."

"Right," Valesa said with a smile. "We serfs have to hang together. Especially if we're Commoners. Let us know if you have any trouble with his lordship, and we'll find some way to make his life miserable."

"I think I can handle that on my own," replied Asteria with a smile.

SEVEN

ooking back later, Asteria found it amazing to think of how quickly she settled into the daily routine. At 0730, just after PT, the academic classes began: first orientation, then a fifteen-minute jog to the next class, Empyrean History I, followed by a fifteen-minute jog to Introductory Mathematics, and finally a free study period, forty-five minutes when the cadets could catch their breath and even talk to one another.

At 1130 came Language Arts; then at 1230 the midday meal (no talking, and you ate what you were served). Afternoon classes began at 1300 with Introductory Biology and continued with Basic Military Organization, Physics, another free study period, and then the day wound up with Alien Life.

Free time—during which cadets were expected to pursue "recreation and constructive activities" or more frequently to pay off any demerits by service on demanding work details—began most days at 1700 and ended at 1800, when they had the evening meal. Finally, at 1845, the cadets were released to their own devices to study, attend meetings of student organizations, send messages home, or simply collapse. They were as free as they could expect to be at the Academy until lights out at 2330. Then they could hope to grab seven and one half hours of sleep before it all began again.

That was the routine for six days out of the week. The fourth and eighth days were given over to athletics, social gatherings, and frantic studying to get ready for the next set of classes. Everyone soon wore a haggard look, including Asteria.

She made no truly close friends. The Aristo girls wouldn't have anything to do with her, and most of the Commoner girls in her barracks had different interests and class schedules. In fact, she really got to know only three of the girls at all well: Valesa Storm, Gala Takeen, and Bren Maddon. Valesa was the only other Commoner girl who had signed up for pilot training. Bala wanted to qualify as a ship's engineer, and Bren was headed for Medical Services. They seemed to like Asteria well enough, but they talked of people and events that Asteria had never even heard of. In the end, Asteria told herself that loneliness was okay. It kept her focused. She wasn't here to socialize.

Unfortunately, Kain Kayser, Count Mastral, was in Asteria's PT class and in two of her other classes. Unlike the other Aristos, he didn't ignore her. Instead he reserved a special kind of cold dislike for her. Not that he ever actually did anything overt—at least nothing that she could definitely blame him for, anyway. But when her equipment was improperly stored ("Three centimeters too close to the front edge of the shelf, Cadet Locke. Take a demerit!"), he was the one who gave her a mocking smirk. And she noticed that in PT he took some care never to be partnered with her in defense training—though he sent his two friends up against her several times. She dealt with them easily enough, but every time they sparred, she noticed how closely Kayser studied her moves.

"He's planning something," Dai warned her when she mentioned this. "His branch of the royal family is made up of schemers and plotters. I know about some of them, because they run the mining operations in the Larenyi asteroid chains—a royal exclusive, you know—so they're rich, but they never think they're rich enough."

Asteria sniffed. "They may be rich, but they're certainly not any good at hand-to-hand combat." Besides, she didn't care. When she sparred with them, all she imagined was fighting against Raiders.

Dai shrugged. "A knife in the back is sneakier than bladehand, but it's a lot more painful."

"He challenged me to fight him in the War Games," Asteria confided.

"You going to?" Dai asked.

"I haven't made up my mind."

"I've signed up," Dai said. "If you're going to do it, deadline is next midbreak."

"I'll think about it. But if I do, Kayser will just think he goaded me into it."

"Let him." Then, grudgingly, Dai added, "I wish his lordship would wash out, but I guess there's no chance of that. He's smart."

Thinking of the special treatment some people seemed to expect—and get—Asteria said scornfully, "He's an Aristo."

"Doesn't make any difference," Dai insisted. "He's carrying a high three right now. Four's the top score. You don't score a 3.7 if you're stupid."

Asteria wasn't fully convinced—virtually all the instructors at the Academy were Commoners, though commissioned officers—and she had seen how deferential they were to Kayser and his peers both inside and outside of class. It wasn't too hard to imagine that now and then the Aristocrats who needed a few extra points got them.

"You'd think that I'd be able to use the extra day of the week to get an edge on him," Asteria said, half to herself. "The week on Theron is Earth Standard, seven days."

Dai laughed. "No one even knows where Earth is anymore," he said. "The first colonists lost track of it five thousand years ago! Why should a week be seven days?"

"It's just what I'm used to," Asteria said. "How long were the weeks on Hovia?"

"We didn't have weeks," he said. "Just days. They started every year with 1 and went to the last day of the year, 402."

Valesa Storm joined them. "We had seven-day weeks on my world, Spar," she said. "Just like on Coriam. That's supposed to be the most Earth-like planet in the Empyrion. I suppose that's why they kept the old Standard seven-day week." She smiled. "I didn't mean to interrupt."

"You're not interrupting," replied Dai with a sigh. "We're all serfs together, right?"

"Right," Valesa said. "Only I don't know how much longer I can stay here. At least not in pilot training. The math is more than I can get." She glanced down at the pulsebook in her hands, frowning.

"What's the problem?" he asked. "Here, let me see...oh, these are vectors. Let me show you how to do this one, and you'll catch on." He bent over her screen. Asteria gazed at the top of his red head and wondered how he could make friends so easily. At times she ached for friendship—she had to admit it—but somehow she didn't have the knack. Back home on Theron, there had been no need for friends; she'd had Andre and her father. But thinking of them only made her ache more.

* * *

The two off days of the eight-day week were Day 4—midbreak, when the afternoons were free—and Day 8, weekbreak, a whole day without classes or duties. On Day 7, each cadet received grades for performance in class. The highest possible grade was 4.0; anything below 2.0 was failing; and the crucial average was 2.5, which would guarantee that a student would not wash out and would allow—eventually—the cadet to receive a few freedoms.

Asteria learned very quickly about the God of 2.5, another statue. It stood at the heart of the campus, on a small island in the center of a round reflecting pool. The nearby buildings were the oldest still standing on campus, some of them constructed more than a thousand years ago. Time had softened their outlines, and vines had crept over their walls until they looked like square, green hills. The pool shimmered like a liquid mirror, reflecting the blue sky.

The statue, made of some dark, eroded stone, was that of the founder of the Academy, His Most Highness Empyrator Sun Volas Kyseros the Fourth, whose ancient ancestors were said to have come from the legendary planet of Earth. He had given the order to organize a special school for educating spacefarers (all students had to be Aristos back then, but that was thousands of years ago). His likeness probably had appeared commanding and regal when new, but after several millennia of weathering, his expression looked grumpy and faintly anxious, like a man suffering from constipation. (Or so Asteria thought with a grin whenever she walked past him.)

He stood on a cylindrical pedestal, staring down at his reflection in the pool, and as students passed by, heading to or from classes (on the double!), they tossed offerings into the water. It was a silly ritual, but everyone believed, or at least said they believed, that it was necessary: "I gave the old man a fifty chip before my math test, and I squeaked out with a 2.51." "I gave him seventy-five before the physics practical, and I aced it!"

The tokens tossed into the pool weren't coins—no one used money here, and there was nothing to buy at the Academy, anyway, because all the necessities were furnished and first-year cadets were not allowed any luxuries. Instead, the offerings were time. At the end of the first month, cadets began to receive time chips as rewards for achievement. You could even trade commendations for chips. Upperclassmen bought favors with them.

Beginning at midterm of freshman year, each chip allowed the cadet a given interval of leave on either midbreak or week-break. They started at ten minutes and went all the way to a thousand minutes. The lower denominations were useless in themselves, but they added up. If you had three hundred minutes in chips, you could extend your half-day leave for five whole hours and not have to report where you were going or what you were doing to anyone. That gave you extra time in the harbor town of Haven, some seventy kilometers from campus, to relax and celebrate.

Most of the gifts tossed to the God of 2.5 were ten-minute chips. Though the first-years couldn't use them until after midterm, they could get their hands on the chips if they were willing to help out a lucky upperclassman with studies, errands, or services—like being a sparring partner for physical conditioning, for instance. You stored them up, because they didn't expire, and hoped that you made Midshipman 4 and could redeem them some day.

Or if you were worried about a test, you tossed one in the pool.

Asteria didn't bother trying to accumulate them, unlike everyone else.

She had no place to go, and no one to go with. The last thing she needed, she thought, was free time. And so the God of 2.5 would receive every chip she got hold of.

Dai had already acquired a ten-minute chip by the first weekbreak day. He tossed it into the pool as he and Asteria passed by on their way to the track. "That's to guarantee a good grade on next week's math test," he called across the water.

"Where'd you get it?" Asteria asked.

"Upperclassman gave it to me because I helped him fix an AI unit he'd broken," Dai said.

"And you threw it away. I mean, I wouldn't keep them, but you're looking forward to going into Haven."

Dai shrugged. "There'll be more. And what's ten minutes, anyway? The place feels deserted, doesn't it?"

Asteria had to agree. All of the eligible upperclassmen had taken off for their leave day, and they passed hardly anyone on their way to the running tracks.

When they arrived at the freshman track, a couple of Aristo boys were just coming off it. "Tamlin!" one of them said cheerfully. "Thanks for the book on early history. I'll get it back to you tomorrow after class."

"No hurry, my lord," Dai said.

"They're not calling you 'Die, Scum' any longer?" asked Asteria as she started to stretch out.

"Some of them are. Some aren't," Dai said, doing knee bends. "Hey, I'm sorry that Kayser and his gang started that 'Disaster' thing. If I'd thought—"

"Don't worry about it," Asteria said. "I don't."

They ran their laps, with Asteria wondering how Dai managed to fit in so well. Aristos and Commoners alike seemed to regard him as...maybe not as a friend, exactly, but as someone they could talk to without insulting. She wished she had his secret.

That evening as Dai, Valesa, and Asteria sat in the common room of Bronze 1 reviewing for a math exam, Kayser came through, glanced at them, and said, "Three freaks of nature. Die, Scum, Disaster, and Total Loss."

Asteria kept her cool. Neither of her friends acknowledged the comment, either, and Kayser went on his way.

Harl Glamis, an Aristo, looked up from his AI screen and called out, "Don't mind Mastral, Dai. Name-calling's the mark of a weak mind."

Asteria started to agree, but Dai stopped her with a hand on her arm and a slight shake of his head. He just nodded pleasantly at Harl.

Harl closed his AI unit and got up.

"When he calls you names, just remember—his cerebral cortex is about the size of a pocknut."

Dai snorted in laughter. "All right, I'll remember," he said. But when Harl strolled away, he muttered, "I shouldn't have laughed. If he tells Kayser, that's just going to make things worse."

"I think Lord Mastral is bad," Valesa half-whispered. "I mean… really bad. Don't you?"

"I try not to think about him at all," Asteria said.

εight

The Academy occupied more than a third of its sprawling subtropical island, though the Space Fleet section of it was far inland. Asteria was used to the wildly varying seasons on Theron, a sharply tilted world. Winters were dark and bleak, with only a couple of hours of sunlight a day, and summers were bright and cool, with twenty hours of light during the warmest part of the year. As her first month ended, she became aware that here there were seasons, too, though they were milder ones. The rainy part of the year set in, with day after day of steady, soaking drizzle. The cadets still ran to classes, but in foul-weather gear: gray for first-years, tan for second-years, dark green for juniors, and royal blue for seniors. Nothing else changed very much.

Somehow during that time of uninterrupted rain, Asteria began to talk with Bren Maddon. They had physical training and their physics class together, and the latter was a complete mystery to Bren. "I'll never get this," she had wailed to Asteria late one evening as they studied in the common room of Bronze 1.

"You just have to get your mind around the equations," Asteria said, more snappishly than she had intended. She bit her lip, sorry that she had caused the other girl to flinch. In a softer tone, she added, "What problem are you on? Okay, that deals with the conservation of momentum. Remember that from class? Now, first we need to determine the vector. Here's how to do that—"

The girls bent over the screen of Asteria's workpad, and Asteria walked her through the process twice. Suddenly, with excitement in her voice, Bren said, "So if there are two objects in an isolated system, if one gains momentum, the other has to lose the same amount?"

"You've got it," Asteria said.

"Now I feel like such a numbhead!" Bren said, tapping her forehead. "Thanks, Dis...I mean, Aster."

"You're welcome. You feel like such a what?"

Bren laughed self-consciously. "Numbhead. Sorry, that's kind of local slang. I come from a Fringe World, and I guess we talk funny."

"I come from a Fringe World too," Asteria said.

"Which one?"

"Theron."

"Oh, yeah, I've heard of it," Bren said, nodding. "That's where the religious fanatics—" She broke off, blushing. "Sorry, Aster."

"That's all right."

"How is Lord Mastral treating you?" Bren asked.

Asteria shrugged. "You see how he avoids me in PT. Outside of class he annoys me. He's got all the Aristos calling me Disaster."

"He's an idiot." Bren blushed. "Don't tell anyone I said that."

"I won't." Asteria flashed a wicked smile. "Just think of what I could make of *his* name!"

"Don't!" Bren said anxiously. "Insulting an Aristo can get you expelled!"

"I won't insult him to his face," said Aster. "But so far I haven't met many Aristos that I like."

In a soft voice, Bren said, "I'm haven't either. Those Aristos—" she broke off, shaking her head.

The two girls looked at each other. Bren was sturdily built, and it wasn't hard to guess that her homeworld was a high-gravity one. "I'll bet you come from Kopenos," Asteria said.

Bren's eyes widened. "I do! How did you know?"

"Just a guess," Asteria told her. She stretched. "Tomorrow's midbreak. Are you going to the War Games?"

"No, I can't." Bren sighed. "I have to study. I'm so far behind! I'm barely hanging on to a 2.6. If I slip—" She didn't finish the sentence.

"I'm not going either," Asteria said. She had finally decided not to sign up for the first-term games—few entering students ever did—and she didn't care to sit in the stands and overhear upper-classmen murmuring snidely about the Commoner in their midst. "If you want, we can have a study session instead. The place ought to be quiet for a couple of hours, anyway. I think you can get the principles of physics—it's just a matter of seeing how they apply."

Bren nodded eagerly. "I'd like that."

* * *

Not a friendship exactly, but Bren was someone to talk to, and someone who shared some of Asteria's feelings and attitudes. "Aristos think they're so great," Bren would mutter. "I mean, it's just an accident of birth."

"I know some Aristos who are pretty bad accidents all by themselves," Asteria growled, thinking of the indolent baron who ran her homeworld and who couldn't be bothered to chase down a band of murderous Raiders.

* * *

Asteria was sitting in the common room the next day proof-reading an upperclassman's history report (the girl from Bronze 2 had assigned her the task when she learned that Asteria wasn't going to the War Games) when a crowd of cadets returned from the arena, chattering and laughing. Valesa Storm ran straight to her. "Did you hear?" she asked.

"Hear what?"

Valesa's face looked stricken. "Dai Tamlin's hurt. He was playing Corona football against Lord Mastral's team—"

Asteria jumped up. "How bad?" she asked, her heart thumping hard.

"Broken wrist, they said, and—where are you going?"

"To sick bay," Asteria called back over her shoulder.

She ran across campus to the medical building where she had received her examination. Before she could ask about Dai, though, she saw him, his face pinched, his left arm in a sling. "Hi," he said, forcing a grin. "I sort of got stomped on." He wiggled the fingers of his left hand.

"What happened?"

He shrugged. "I caught a pass in the last minute of the game. If I'd scored, we would've won, but Lord Mastral and his friend Broyden stopped me. They really piled on."

"And you broke your wrist when you fell?"

Dai shook his head. "I was trying to hold onto the ball so it wouldn't be counted as a fumble. Broyden hunched over me,

94

and Lord Mastral stamped on my hand. The referees didn't see it."

"You've got to report that!" Asteria whispered.

"No use. I can't prove it. And Broyden and Mastral are Aristos. A court-martial would believe their word over a Commoner's. Let's get back to the barracks. They've given me something to make my bones heal faster, and I don't feel so great."

They walked back through the darkening evening. "So you lost?" she asked.

"Yeah, by three points. If I'd scored—"

"If you'd scored," interrupted a sneering voice from the shadows, "you would have been a halfway decent player instead of a loser."

Asteria felt a jolt from her belt, felt all her muscles tighten. "Kayser, shut up," she snapped.

"You will address me as 'my lord,' you Commoner filth," Kayser said, stepping out of the shadow. Broyden and Gull flanked him.

"Come on, relax," Dai said uneasily.

"Dai told me how you cheated," Asteria hissed.

Kayser smirked. "At least I played. You were too much of a coward to go out for the games," he said. "I wanted to show you what would have happened to you. You want to fight me, Disaster? There are three of us and only one of you."

"Two," Dai said. "And I'm right-handed, my lord, so this wrist won't be a problem."

Kayser's eyes darted from Asteria to Dai and back again. "We'll break the other one this time," he said. Then he snapped, "Get them!"

Both Broyden and Gull had seen Asteria in action, and they stepped forward slowly and reluctantly. The power from the belt seemed to fill Asteria like liquid fire. Again, she had the strange sense that things were moving in slow motion. Broyden was nearer. She dropped, braced on her arm, and did a full leg sweep, catching him at the ankles and sending him toppling. Before he had hit, she sprang upright, feinted so that Gull's quick blow whooshed harmlessly past her cheek, and uphanded his chin, stunning him and sending him reeling against Kayser, who had stepped back.

"Get off me!" Kayser shrieked, shoving Gull to the side.

"Come on," Asteria said.

Kayser looked down at Broyden, who was gripping his ankle and who looked as if he wasn't even considering getting up. Gull staggered, turned, and ran.

Kayser's lip curled. "I'll let you off this time. You could be expelled for touching me, Disaster. You remember that! Come on, idiot!" He turned and strode away. Broyden got up and followed him with an exaggerated limp.

"Always fun at the Royal Military Academy," Dai muttered.

"Next time," Asteria growled, "I think I *will* go out for the War Games."

* * *

As the term went on, the rains began to break up—instead of raining twenty-six hours a day, now it rained for only twenty. Occasionally, the nights were even clear enough of clouds for the other suns of the Corona to show up in the dark sky as a cluster of brilliant stars. Coriam, the homeworld of the

Corona Aristocrats, showed up as a shining blue planet, so near that it was visible as a minute blue disk. It was the third world in the system, and rumor said that it was a cool planet, with dark seas and tall mountains capped with shining white snow. Not that a Commoner would ever be likely to see them in person.

A week before midterm, Asteria had racked up a 3.1 average, and Dai had barely edged her out—3.13. "I'd do better than that if I didn't have chemistry," she complained. "I've got a 3.8 in PT."

"Because you have those crazy reflexes," complained Dai. It was weekbreak, and the two of them were hiding out in a study room of the library—if they showed their faces on campus, some upperclassman was sure to yell for them to do something: run to the barracks for a piece of sports equipment, a thendel racquet or a fieldball glove, or return some pulsebooks to the library, or even proofread and correct homework. Dai sprawled in his chair. "I still don't know how you manage to progress at the speed you do. What are you bench-pressing now?"

"Fifty-five K, standardized."

He grimaced. "I'm up by exactly half a kilo. How do you do it?"

"I don't know." The truth was, however, she was beginning to suspect there was more to her steady gain in physical strength than just training. She knew it wasn't the food they were given—it was supposed to meet all nutritional standards, but judging from the taste, it probably had about as many vitamins as sawdust.

"As long as I hold a 3.0 or better, I'm not worrying," Dai said.

"Why a 3.0?" asked Asteria with a smile. "Don't you make offerings to the God of 2.5?"

"Sure," he said, grinning. "I'm no heathen. But I've signed on for the third term in space. While the Aristos are having summer break, I intend to be serving on a Fleet ship."

"I signed up too," Asteria said. "I didn't know about the grade requirement."

"It's just for first-years," Dai told her. "After that, 2.5 is good enough. Not many first-year students sign on, though."

"Why not? Space experience—"

"We're serfs," he reminded her. "For us, space experience is going to be doing the work even Cybots object to doing. Aristos don't like getting their fingers dirty."

"I'm not afraid of work," Asteria said. "Summer can't come too fast for me."

"Time does seem to fly by when you're having fun," Dai agreed with a grin, flexing his nearly healed wrist. "Six more days to midterm." He stretched and yawned. "And then we can get away from this zoo for half a day once a month. And at least we'll be out of orientation after midterm. We'll have study period instead for two days a week and pilot pre-training for the other four. Have you ever flown a ship?"

She shook her head. "Not a spaceship. Dad let me handle the controls of a skimmer once or twice. Not takeoffs or landings, but cruising. It's not the same."

"No, it isn't," Dai agreed wryly. "Anyhow, there's one subject where I've got the edge on you. I've flown an orbiter...umm, twice. Took off, docked, and landed."

"You couldn't have been old enough."

"Sure I was," Dai insisted. "I lived through it, didn't I?"

Asteria's hands itched to be at the controls of a real spaceship. "I thought you had to be licensed, and you can't get a license until you're seventeen."

Dai shrugged. "I'd had lots of simulator hours already. And flying a real ship—well, Dad was kind of loose about that—and anyway, my uncle was along in the pilot's seat. I was just copiloting, but he let me handle everything. Almost everything. He did the fine controls on the docking maneuver."

Asteria was only half-listening to Dai's chatter. "What will pre-training be like?" she asked aloud.

Dai scratched his nose thoughtfully, and in the light of the study cubicle, Asteria noticed that his red hair seemed a little more intense in color than it had on the *Stinger*. Of course, he had bulked up a little too—despite Dai's complaints, no one could go through six hours of intensive PT a week without adding muscle. He yawned again—he always seemed starved for sleep—and said, "I hear you start out with the physics and math of spaceflight for three days, and the fourth day is simulator time. Next term, it's two days of classroom, two days on the sim. And before we move up to Midship 2, we'll each have logged five hours of real flight time in trainers. You give up midbreak for that, but it's worth it."

He seemed excited by the prospect. Asteria thought about flying. It wasn't piloting, not Space Fleet flying, but something like a merger of pilot and craft. Skimmer pilots sat in a command seat and operated hand controls, but not Space Fleet captains. She had always thought such piloting seemed exciting, and she still wanted to see what it was like...but somehow her enthusiasm had faded.

What's wrong with me? It was hard to get through the days, knowing that each class was going to be a challenge. It was harder to get through the nights, dreaming about her father and her cousin. Asteria felt drawn, weary, dulled by routine. She hoped flight training would spark some life deep inside her. Lately she had begun to wonder if all this was worth it—the long hours, the constant rain of insults and orders from upperclass cadets, the demanding teachers, and the relentless tide of work. She had wanted to become a pilot to pay back the Raiders for what they had done to her family—but it would take four long years for her to earn her pilot's seat. Revenge was going to be a very cold dish.

"I was reading about your dad just yesterday," Dai said suddenly. "*The History of the Tetraploid Wars*. There's a whole chapter about the *Adastra*. It mentioned your dad's name as one of the badly wounded."

"Yes," Asteria said flatly. "He was hurt."

Dai frowned. "It said—I'm sorry, I shouldn't even be—"

"No, it's all right," Asteria interrupted, softening her tone. She thought of the ridiculous statue on campus, the heroic Aristocrat supporting the gruesomely wounded Commoner. "What did it say?"

Slowly, Dai replied, "It said that he was so badly hurt that the doctors wanted to harvest his nervous system and implant it in a Cybot. But he wouldn't let them. So they did a massive reconstruction. It said your father's surgeries pioneered three new types of cybernetic implants."

Asteria nodded, her throat tight. "That sounds about right. One of his eyes was a cyber unit, one of his legs, and an arm from the elbow down."

"I'm sorry."

She swallowed. "I grew up knowing him like that. He didn't let it bother him," she said. "I think…never mind."

"What?"

"Nothing."

"Come on," he said. "No secrets, all right? We're fellow Commoners here."

Asteria took a deep breath. "I think he would have stayed in the Space Fleet if they'd let him," she said. "I don't believe he ever wanted to be anything else. Not a farmer. Not—not anything. The way he talked about the Fleet—it was home to him. But too many people in the Fleet would have talked to him about what he did during the attack, and the Aristo who brought the ship back to port didn't want him talking. So they made a deal. The Fleet patched Dad up, and he agreed to keep it all to himself in exchange for a land grant. He settled for a life as a farmer. And as my dad."

"That's not exactly settling," Dai said shyly. "Uh, I mean he sounds like a good man."

"He was," said Asteria. She felt like crying. She turned away from Dai and dimly realized that in their brief conversation something in her life had shifted permanently.

They left the library and went to dinner. After the meal, as the cadets were scattering back to their dorms. Dai and Asteria walked back to Bronze 1 together. Darkness had fallen, and they took one of their usual shortcuts. It led past the reflecting pool.

Asteria, deep in thought, barely heard Dai talking. "What?"

"I said, 'What's that humming?'" Dai responded. He was only a dark silhouette, but Aster could see that his head was cocked.

Asteria stopped in her tracks. She heard it too, a faint buzzing that seemed to come from somewhere overhead. "I don't know—"

But at that moment, she felt the tingling jolt of energy that her belt gave her whenever she felt threatened. Her senses sharpened. She jerked her head around and saw something vague and small hovering a couple of meters off the ground, over above the pool.

She heard quick footsteps.

"Watch out," she cautioned, pivoting.

"Disaster and Die, Scum," spat Kayser, melting out of the darkness. "Are you two in love?"

"We're not bothering you," Asteria said.

"Come on and fight me, why don't you?" Kayser asked mockingly.

"Don't do it," Dai warned.

"Don't do it," Kayser said, mimicking Dai's tone in a sing-song lilt. "Coward. Come on, Disaster. I don't have my friends around now. Come on and try me. There's nobody here to witness it, is there?"

Asteria almost went for him. But then she thought twice, backed away, stooped quickly, and picked up a round stone from the border of the pool. "Is there?" she asked.

Kayser flinched as she spun and with a deadly accurate overhand throw whipped the stone out over the pool. It crashed against something hovering in the air—and it splashed down.

"Now there isn't," she said. "You had a camera bot focused on us! Was it taking infrared photos, Kayser? You wanted me to hit you, and you'd have the photos to prove it. All right—let's fight!"

Kayser turned to run.

"Are you leaving, my lord?" asked a voice from the darkness.

"We think you should stay," another said.

With her heightened senses, Asteria stared into the shadows—and relaxed. The newcomers were Valesa and Bren. And they blocked Kayser's only line of retreat.

His voice became high-pitched: "If you even touch me, you'll be expelled!"

"I don't think so," Dai said. "Your cambot's in the water. It's your word against ours—and now there are four of us."

"This isn't fair," Kayser yowled.

"Relax," Asteria said, struggling against the urge to fight him there and then to end it. "Listen, let's make a truce."

Bren and Valesa had closed in. Kayser shifted. "Wh-what do you mean, a truce?" he stammered.

"I mean you need to drop this feud," Asteria said firmly. "We're both trying to make it at the Academy. You don't need me giving you trouble, and I don't need any trouble from you."

Kayser was silent.

"It's a good offer," Dai said before adding, "my lord."

The silence stretched out. Bren said impatiently, "He's not going to agree, Aster. Let's—"

"I'll agree," Kayser said hastily. "All right, all right, I'll agree. Now let me go!"

"Just a moment," Dai said. "Let's understand each other. Asteria agrees that she won't humiliate you in front of your friends. You have to agree to the same. You won't call her Disaster any longer."

"I don't care what he calls me," Asteria said sharply.

"Then that doesn't matter," Dai continued smoothly. "But this does. You won't try to trick her into fighting you. In fact, you'll treat her just as you would an Aristo. My lord."

"If she'll let me alone, I'll let her alone," Kayser said coldly. "Does that satisfy you?"

"Yes," Asteria said. "Let him go."

Kayser didn't quite run away, but he hurried off in the dark—at double time.

Bren and Valesa laughed. "That's taken care of," Bren said.

"If he'll live up to it," Valesa said.

Asteria nodded. "I think he will."

"He might find it hard to forgive Asteria's shot at his little toy. Cambots are expensive," Dai said.

"He won't mind losing it," Bren told him. "Aristos have lots of money."

"No," Dai said. "I meant thanks to Cadet Kayser, Asteria just gave the God of 2.5 the biggest offering he ever had!"

Asteria's heart was pumping hard. She still felt the keen lift the belt gave her in moments of crisis.

"Come on," Bren said. "Time we got back to the barracks."

Asteria forced herself to take deep breaths. "I'm with you." And just then, in the dark, she knew that it didn't matter if it took her four years to become a pilot.

She would do it.

And somehow, some day—

She would find the Raiders and make them suffer.

ΠΙΠΕ

"Υ ou can't take it off?" the tech asked, staring at the silvery belt.
"It's a medical device," Asteria told him. "I have a special waiver." She wished he would hurry up and spray on her suit. Though for all his visible reaction, she might have been one of the statues on campus, not a girl standing barefoot and wearing only her underwear.

The tech shook his head doubtfully. "I'll have to check."

Asteria held out her wrist, and he scanned her link. "See?"

"Okay," he said reluctantly. "I guess. But I've never sprayed a pressure suit over something like that before. Get into the chamber."

Asteria's heart was hammering. At last! It was spring term, and she had made the grade of Midshipman 2 along with Dai and 90 percent of the entering class. Ten percent had washed out—or quit—before the end of their first term. Now, after weeks of working in the class and in simulators, she was going to be at the controls of a real ship.

She stepped onto the circular pad, and the tech lowered the clear cylinder down over her. "Stand straight," he warned uselessly. She couldn't stand any straighter. She had a moment of panicky uncertainty when the cylinder bonded to the pad, a little flutter of claustrophobia. "Hold your breath," the tech said, his voice sounding hollow. Asteria took a deep breath and held it. "Close your eyes."

She did, heard a hiss, and felt the misting spray of the first coating. Then a circle rose from the floor, up over her feet. It looked like a bubble wand—she peeked—with a white translucent liquid trapped in it. The liquid coated her body, drying instantly with a strange cooling effect. She spread her fingers and felt the stuff flow on like gloves, then up to her neck. It stopped at her chin. The circle sank back down into the pad. The seal hissed, and the cylinder lifted away.

A frosted Asteria stepped off the pad, wearing her pressure suit. It fit tightly, like a second skin. "The helmet has neural transceivers built in," the tech said, handing it to her. "Put it on and let me bond it. You'll think you can't breathe, but don't worry—the suit is oxygenating your blood. And you don't have to talk. Just subvocalize—"

"I know," she said, slipping the helmet on. She held her breath—easier if she opened her mouth—and waited as the tech went round her neck with a spray and then did it again to make sure the suit was really airtight.

"Test it," the tech said. "What's your name?"

She let her vocal cords form the words "Aster Locke," and heard a depersonalized voice that came from the helmet repeat the words aloud.

"Right, you're set. Through there." The tech touched a control pad, and two doors dissolved. Asteria went through the one that he pointed toward as another cadet, stripped to his underwear, entered the suiting chamber.

Twenty flight cadets waited, milling around, speaking to one another in those flat, identical-sounding suit voices. They all looked as if their bodies had been wrapped in plastic. She couldn't recognize them—the helmets all had a gold faceplate, opaque from the outside. The names of the cadets were displayed on the foreheads, though. Mastral was there. Asteria looked for Dai but couldn't spot him. He might have been one of the last five, though.

The door dissolved again, and everyone looked around as the twenty-first suited cadet entered—Kayser's friend Broyden, Asteria saw from his name display. Beyond him, she caught a glimpse of red hair and relaxed. Dai would be the next in line. Broyden walked past her, craning his head, as if he had an urgent need to find Kayser. "Mastral?" his strange machine voice said.

"Here."

The others were talking, but Asteria had no one to talk to. She heard a contemptuous "Disaster," though, and knew it had to be Kayser. Though he had not dropped the nickname, he had at least kept his word about not harassing her—so far. True, he had crowed at the beginning of the term that he had beaten her out—and it was also true that she had earned a 3.11 grade average, while he had a 3.12, thanks either to his greater skill at chemistry or to favoritism. Still, he had stopped trying to taunt her into striking him—although he had never again faced her in defense training. And she was determined that he was not going to best her in flight training.

Dai came in and immediately saw her. "Feels weird not breathing," he said, his voice flat as the suit picked up his sub-vocalization and turned it into mechanical speech.

"Yeah, it does," she agreed. "You sound like a Cybot."

"So do you."

Asteria had to keep conscious control of her lungs, because the moment she forgot about them, she felt herself clenching and gasping to breathe—no need, because the suit was infiltrating her blood with oxygen, the amount automatically determined by her level of exertion. "This is it," she said.

"Yeah," Dai agreed. "You don't have to worry, though. You're great on the sims."

She didn't respond, though it was true—she was the best in her class on the simulators, her reflexes like lightning. The final three cadets came in. As soon as the last one had stepped into the ready room, the opposite door dissolved, and a flight sergeant said, "To your ships."

The trainers looked impossibly small, not even as large as—well, as a coffin. They were all jet-black and shining, symmetrical flattened tubes, open at the moment, waiting for their pilots. Twelve on each side of the hangar, one at the far end of the row. The sergeant sent the cadets in: first Kayser, who went to the end ship, and then two at a time. Dai and Asteria walked down the row together, not quite to the middle, and he turned to take the left ship as Asteria turned to the right. "Good luck," he said.

"You too."

It was just like the sim, except that there they had not worn the strange suits, just the helmet. Asteria stepped into the trainer and then lay back. The ship clamshell shut over her, and she felt the pressure as the contacts expanded, locking her into place. At first, everything was dark. Then, suddenly, she could see more than she had ever seen in her life. The faceplate had interlocked with the ship sensors.

She saw in visible light, infrared, and ultraviolet. She could, just by thinking about it, see everything surrounding the ship simultaneously, 360-degree vision. The ship introduced itself. "Trainer Seven."

"This is neat," said a voice in her ear—Dai's voice, sounding more like himself now that it was transmitted through the ship instead of just through the suit.

"Silence, Trainer Eight," came the voice of the flight sergeant. "No ship-to-ship conversation until you're in flight."

"Give him a demerit." Kayser's voice, of course.

"Then you'd get one as well, Trainer One. Last warning. Silence."

Asteria closed her eyes and felt the ship. The connections were pulsing through her skin and directly into her nervous system. Ages ago, pilots had controlled flight mechanically—how, she had no idea. It seemed impossibly complex to think about. Now they *felt* the ship. No need for dials and readouts, because the information came directly into the pilot's mind, the way a pulse-book transmitted information directly to the cortex.

These were suborbital, little more than skimmers, but they had the most sophisticated flight controls that Asteria had ever dealt with. Equipped with grav drives—no rockets, no ion exhaust, just a high-pitched shriek—they used gravity waves to take to the air and streak along at supersonic speeds. Each one was powered for two hours of flight, and if a student was so unlucky as to be at top altitude—one hundred kilometers—when the power reached 2 percent, then the ship's AI would take over and bring them down for a soft landing. Maybe not on the actual campus, but somewhere.

Or so the theory went. Everyone knew stories of cadets who had miscalculated, lost control, and crashed. A few of them were buried on campus.

"Right," the flight sergeant's voice boomed. "Your solos today are to Grayhorn Mountain, then to the Bight of Westfall, and then back here. Only five hundred kilometers. You have two hours, so keep your speed reasonable. This is not a race. Make sure you register with the detectors at Grayhorn and the Bight. Lay in your courses."

Thinking *Grayhorn* did nothing. Asteria smiled to herself. This must be one of the little tricks they liked to pull on first-timers. But she had prepared. She thought *Latitude 30.102, Longitude 1.348*, and before her she saw a map of the island shimmering in midair. She willed the ship to calculate the most direct flight path to the coordinates she had given it—to Grayhorn, then to the Bight, seventy-five odd kilometers to the south, and then a direct route back to the hangar. It was, she saw, a total of 147.812 kilometers. Close enough to the FS's estimate of one-fifty.

From there, she calculated the speeds, the turns required, and the time involved. Gave herself half an hour buffer. Before she knew it, she heard the FS say, "Trainer One, clear. Go! Trainer Two, clear. Go!"

Right down the line. When the DS called for Trainer Seven, she had already engaged the grav drive. At the go command, the ship sprang five meters into the air, swiveled, and shot down the length of the hangar, through the arched exit, and soared in a high climbing starboard curve. For the first time in months, Asteria felt like laughing. She could see *everything!* The ship rolled so the landscape of the campus shot by below her. Behind her, the blue sky went up forever. She could hear, very faintly, ship-to-ship chatter now that seven ships were airborne. No, eight—there was Dai's voice: "Where are you?"

"Ten klicks south of you already. I can see you, barely."

"Got you now. Wanna race?"

"No way I'm slowing! Catch me if you can!"

"Cut the chatter," said the voice of Command. "Remember we can hear you. Communicate only when necessary."

"Aye," said Dai and Asteria in unison.

Away from the campus the unbroken canopy of island jungle flashed past two kilometers below, a deep green tinged with blue. Flickers of discharge sheeted around the ship, pale violets and reds. Asteria couldn't hear it, but she knew the ship was shrieking, as if it felt the joy of flight just as she did.

Then the vision feed failed.

"Dai!"

"Malfunction?"

"No viz," she said. "Command? I've—"

"Don't," Dai said quickly. "It's a test. The ships are programmed to do that. I've lost some rear stabilizer control. The turns are gonna be wide."

Give me virtual plotting, Asteria thought. Instantly, she saw the world in a kind of sketch: the scarlet horizon line ringed her, moving green dots showed her the trainers ahead of her and behind her. Her speed had faltered with the surprise, and Dai had closed to within five kilometers of her. *Superimpose map.* Now in yellow she saw the physical features of the course: a river wound through the jungle below. In the far distance, Grayhorn showed up as an inverted yellow V. She adjusted course and speed and headed for it flat-out.

"What's your hurry?" asked Dai.

"I've decided it is a race after all," Asteria told him.

"Watch your communications," Command warned again, but the voice sounded faintly amused.

She passed Trainer Six.

"What are you doing?" the cadet pilot asked.

She didn't bother to respond. Now her altitude readout was behaving weirdly. It indicated she was within ten meters of the jungle canopy, though she knew she had maintained a two-kilometer altitude and that number had to be wrong.

Time zipped by as she fought with blindness. She caught up with Trainer Five, and then without warning, visual came back. She saw the ancient bare black rock of Grayhorn's conical volcano and, beyond that, the silver glint of the sea. Now she was abreast of Trainer Four, Broyden. "Who's that?" he asked. "I'm reporting you for violating approach distances!"

She checked the readout. She was more than the required kilometer away from him, so she ignored the threat. Now Grayhorn loomed before her, and she was calculating turn vectors. She whipped the trainer around in so tight an arc that she felt the G forces build up even though the grav drive was supposed to muffle them. She was aware of a ping from the transceiver on Grayhorn, and she downloaded a pulse to it, verifying her arrival—but already the mountain lay behind her, and she was streaking for the seacoast and the Bight, an enormous round crater now filled with water, former home to an ancient volcano that must have rivaled Grayhorn.

Ahead of her, Trainer Three looked as if it were in trouble. Instead of level flight, it rolled, turning over and over. As she caught up to it, she transmitted advice: "Don't fight it. Bank to port and ascend at ten meters per second. That'll straighten it out."

No response, so she could only hope the struggling cadet had registered what she had sent. The waters of the Bight lay ahead now, turquoise, streaked with white waves. A ping, and she downloaded the proof of her passing, took a hard climbing bank, and set course for the campus and the hangar.

"Elapsed time?" she asked.

The ship told her that she had been in flight for fifty-seven minutes and forty-one seconds. Incredible. It had felt like ten minutes.

And it also felt...*hot.* Great, now the enviros were malfunctioning. She took a suit temp reading and found it was up to thirty-four, nearly body temperature. Sweat could interfere with the suit's transpiration, leaving her short of oxygen. She wondered if she had pushed the ship too hard. Or was it another test of how she would react? Best not to obsess over it. There was Trainer Two, not far ahead. She overtook and passed it. Now Kayser was out there somewhere...there! She urged the trainer to a higher speed.

"Who's that?" Kayser asked in an annoyed voice.

"My name is Aster," she told him. "You don't seem to have the brains to remember it."

"You're not supposed to be racing!"

"Who said I was? I just like the feeling of speed." Asteria waited for Command to reprimand her, but evidently,

113

whoever was monitoring the transmissions didn't feel called upon to scold.

Kayser's trainer shot forward, accelerating at close to its top limit. Asteria grinned and let her own vessel go, pushing it to full speed. "Move over, Kayser. I'm coming through."

"That's a demerit!" he snapped. "You can't call me that!"

She chose not to answer. They had to turn now—their speed was taking them off course. Though they were moving at the same rate, Asteria had the inside of the turn, unless Kayser had the courage to strain the trainer past its design tolerances. That meant she could pass him. Keeping to the razor edge of thrust failure, Asteria kept the craft in a tight turn. She came abreast of Kayser's craft. She was pulling ahead—

Power supply at 5 percent, the ship told her sternly. Instantly, she consulted the datafeeds. She wouldn't make it, not at this speed. Ten kilometers short of the hangar the ship would take over and land itself. How many demerits would that cost her?

Unless—

Unless it was another test, a trick. Doing a quick calculation in her head, she thought she should have more power than that—25 percent at least. Should she slow?

Warning: Power supply at 4 percent. Ship override in two minutes.

She could slow to half speed and make it. Or she could chance it and—

"I'm out of power!" Kayser's panicky voice sliced through her thoughts. "The ship's taking me down!"

She couldn't see him. She was too far ahead. But if he was out of power, her ship might be out too—

She reduced thrust to half speed. She would come in with seconds to spare now. Already, she could see the campus in the distance. She calculated her incoming trajectory and made a course adjustment to use the absolute minimum of power. She was over the main entrance of the campus now at only five hundred meters altitude. People were staring up. There was the hangar—

A black blur screamed past her. "Sorry, Disaster—"

Asteria's blood ran cold at his snickering. Kayser had slowed and was already entering the hangar. She guided her trainer in ten seconds after him. She slipped into the correct berth and released the hatch. The flight sergeant was waiting, his face purple.

"What did I tell you?" he demanded.

"I kept to within tolerances," Asteria told him, climbing out.

"Stand still." He released the sleek helmet and helped her lift it off. "Breathe!"

She gasped air and felt woozy. At the far end of the trainer dock, two helpers had removed Kayser's helmet. He came swaggering toward them. "Sergeant," he said, "I want to report this cadet. She improperly addressed me by my family name."

The sergeant glared at him. "If I give her a demerit, my lord, you must have two. We could hear your transmissions. You deliberately violated your orders when you engaged in a race with Trainer Seven. You transmitted false data to her craft."

Kayser's face turned scarlet. "I didn't do—"

"Please!" The sergeant leaned close, and in a furious, low voice, he said, "You didn't do anything? I was listening, my lord! You overrode the data stream in Trainer Seven to make it look as though it was out of power. And you sent a false distress communication. Both are against the rules. Now—do you want to press your charge?"

"No, let it go," Kayser snapped and stalked past Asteria. The doorway swallowed him.

A moment later, Trainer Two swooped in and berthed. Hot on its tail was Trainer Three. Asteria reported to the tech who had suited her, and he removed the pressure suit in the same efficient fashion. "If you get short of breath, use this," he said, handing her a respirator no longer than her little finger. "It's triox. You may have to use it to adjust to breathing on your own the first few times you suit up. All right, get into your uniform and then report to Sigma Two for debriefing."

Four other girls had been on the training flight, and the last of them, an Aristo named Gaila, came in as Asteria finished dressing. "Mastral will have your skin," she warned in passing. "Remember you're a Commoner." Her mouth curled in what might have been a smile. "Even if you do know how to fly."

By the time the class had assembled in the debriefing hall, Kayser had told everyone about beating Asteria in their impulsive race. Asteria clenched her teeth. So much for their truce. She didn't like the way Kayser's cronies grinned at her, but what did she expect?

The flight coordinator came in, ran through the list of cadets, and explained what they had done right and had done wrong. Some had been slow to react to deliberate complications; others had made errors in navigation—one, a hapless Aristo named Mikkels, had come back half an hour late after making a bad turn, not realizing the obvious—that his nav system was giving him false data.

Still, everyone scraped through with grades of 2.5 or better. Dai's was a very respectable 3.0. Asteria's was 3.4—"You reacted well to the onboard emergencies," the coordinator observed dryly. "Almost well enough to rack up a perfect 4.0. But you exceeded the speed requirements in returning."

Her face felt hot when Kayser received a score of 3.7. "You received a 3.4 for your navigation and reaction to emergency situations," the flight coordinator said. "And we decided to give you a 10 percent bonus for having won an informal race."

Kayser flashed Asteria a triumphant leer.

Dai whispered, "Don't react."

As the class broke up, Kayser and his shadow Broyden strutted past. Asteria said, "Congratulations on winning the high score... my Lord Mastral."

He stared coldly at her. "That's not funny, Disaster." To Broyden, he said, "I don't think she'll be at the Academy much longer. Too gullible."

Only after the two had left the hangar did Asteria realize she had balled her hands into fists.

"Let them laugh," Dai told her. "You can show him up at the end of term in the War Games. Hey, want to go into Haven this weekbreak?"

"No." Alone of all the students who had earned the average of 2.5, Asteria had never left the campus for the monthly half-day excursion to the coastal town.

"Come on," Dai said. "Get some real food for a change. Swim in the sea."

"I don't have any money," Aster said.

"I thought they were supposed to give you an allowance from your father's estate."

"Oh, they will. Eventually. The Bourse don't do anything quickly."

"Then I'll treat."

"No, thanks. I just don't want to, all right?" She hesitated when Dai dropped behind. "What's wrong?"

Dai was huffing and puffing for air. She turned and saw that his complexion had taken on a faint green tinge. He tried to smile. It looked like a grin of pain. He gasped, "Uh—are you going to use your triox?"

"Turned it in already," she said.

"Oh."

"Come on," she told him. "You're just readjusting to the air, that's all. Using two triox would be a rules violation."

"Right." But he gave her an odd look, and he sounded far from convinced that she was sincere about "rules."

ten

ar Games.
Asteria had heard of them almost as soon as she set foot on Academy soil. They happened every year, toward the end of spring term. For sixteen days, classes were suspended, students dropped all talk about ways to violate rules without being caught, and the instructors became intensely interested in advising their favorite cadets on how to conduct themselves.

The first-year cadets were also first in the War Games schedule. The four hundred top-ranked cadet pilots were divided up into sixteen teams for the competition. On the first day, by an arbitrary selection process, each team was paired with an enemy team. The eight winners went on to a second pairing on the second day; on the third day, the surviving four were paired; and on the last day, the surviving two teams faced each other for the top honor of the class.

The teams alternated between playing the roles of attacker or defender in each round. Defenders would be given a specific task—prevent the enemy ships from knocking out a communications center, for example, represented by a beacon that could be silenced if an attacking ship could hit a target with a laser beam. The attackers had to devise the strategy and tactics necessary to achieve their objective.

And of course the flight coordinators would be sure to throw in challenging accidents and mishaps. Asteria and Dai both made the cut, though they were not assigned to the same team, somewhat to Asteria's disappointment. She was in Team Gold, he in Team Red. The Golds, led by an Aristo girl named Helene Kaccia (merely the daughter of a baron, and so no one had to call her "my lady"), had informally decided to rename themselves the Bolts, and they adopted a stylized jagged spear of lightning as their symbol. Dai was the leader of the Reds, and Asteria wasn't surprised (and admittedly, she was amused) to hear that he had decided to call his team the Fabulous Flying Freaks. Their symbol was a brick.

"Why a brick?" she'd asked him.

Dai shrugged. "Why not?"

Kayser was the commander of the Silver team—he had renamed them the Daggers—and Asteria suspected that he must have used his Aristo influence, because Broyden and Gull, his two buddies, were also on his team.

Helene was on edge about the contest. "We may not win," she said, "but please, please, *please*, let's make it to the third round at least. You're all good—but make sure you're at least that much better than the other teams. If we get to round three, no one's going to make fun of us."

The first day was not very challenging at all. The Bolts were paired against the Sabers, with the Bolts attacking, the Sabers defending. They flew trainers almost identical to the one Asteria had first flown—only these were equipped with mock weapons, chiefly laser cannons. They fired harmless light, but any ship hit by the blast would register the probable damage and relay the score to flight control.

Their turn came early in the morning. Already Asteria had seen Dai, who triumphantly announced that the Freaks had soundly trounced the Team Green. Charged with defending a section of airspace, the Freaks had engaged the Green ships in close aerial combat, losing nine ships to imaginary damage but downing or seriously damaging all twenty-five of the enemy.

Asteria suited up for the briefing. Helene told them they were protecting a troop transport, represented by a huge, slow skimmer. They had to see it safely across two hundred kilometers of airspace to win. She divided the pilots up, with some taking positions below the skimmer, some to either side, and some above. To Asteria, Helene said, "I want you to fly rear guard. Hang back, be inconspicuous, and charge in if anyone gets in trouble."

"Aye," Asteria replied.

Helene gave her a wan smile. "You've got good moves, Locke. Not all Aristos think you're a disaster."

"Thank you, group leader," Asteria said flatly.

They took off, assumed positions around the lumbering skimmer, and Helene gave the order to arm their weapons. Everyone reported in, Asteria last as the rear guard—and before Asteria knew it, they were gaining altitude as they left the Academy behind.

She kept her senses on the alert. A hundred kilometers out, she spotted the first attack, a wave of six ships coming in high from the north. And when the others were fighting them off, she saw the second wing, rising one at a time from the dark cleft canyon of a river far below. "Straight ahead and low!" she said over the ship-to-ship communicator. "This is the main body!"

"Gold three, four, five, six, and seven, engage!" Helene ordered. "Nine, ten, eleven, twelve, thirteen, give them support!"

The Gold team swooped down like hawks. Asteria counted ten enemy ships down on the deck. Six overhead…there were still nine to account for. Not behind, not ahead…not above or below. The trainer pulsed data to her as the trainers wheeled and fired their laser markers at each other: "Saber seventeen disabled. Saber nineteen destroyed. Gold three, 12 percent damage, life support marginal. Saber two disabled."

"Here they come," Asteria said. "The last nine: high and dead ahead."

"Gold twenty-four and twenty-five, stay with the troop carrier," Helene ordered. "Everyone else, come with me!"

Below, the trainers that had been downed were skimming off on autopilot, their human pilots unable to affect them now. Three of the Gold ships had been destroyed or damaged so badly they were out of the battle, but on the other hand, fourteen of the Sabers had been put out of commission. The Sabers had only eleven left. Still, even one would be enough—if the pilot's aim was true. "Heads up!" snapped Asteria. "Get him, get him!"

That fantastic 360-degree vision flooded her head, showing her everything that was happening. The lead Saber ship had rolled out of combat and was diving down on the transport. Pako Zanthem, an Aristo boy whose nerve seemed cold as liquid nitrogen, rose to meet it—but almost at once Asteria's trainer said, "Gold twenty-four pilot killed," and Zanthem's ship dived away.

The belt cut in, boosting her awareness, speeding her reaction so that time slowed down. Asteria warped her own trainer up to face the threat. She yawed, letting the enemy laser bursts beam past harmlessly, then focused on its leading edge, where the pilot's head would be. The Saber ship did a tricky bank, but she stuck with it and fired her weapons. "Saber one downed," Asteria's trainer told her. She spun to get back to the transporter they were protecting, and then she saw another enemy ship closing fast.

She pounced on it and fired; a half-second later it fired back; and the trainer announced, "Saber four navigation disabled. No score on Saber four's firing." Adrenaline course through her as she rose again—

Then it was all over. Just like that. The voice of a controller said, "Well done, Gold. Decision by massacre. All trainers return to base."

She felt the heightened awareness drain away as the formation peeled off to retrace its course. The belt's effect faded, leaving her feeling empty.

After the return to the Academy and the debriefing, Asteria found Dai watching two other mock battles in the barracks holoroom. "This real time?" she asked, sitting next to him.

"Virtual but close. There's his highness." Dai pointed at a pair of shimmering silver arrowheads that appeared to glide a few centimeters over the screen. "Silver's attacking, trying to break through the Indigo lines to destroy a power grid. The main battle's over there. Kayser faked being hit—don't know why, but the controller didn't call it so nobody would be fooled—and dropped back, then swung around. His wingman's Gull. The Indigo defense is pretty tight...and there are four ships orbiting the grid center—that's the yellow beacon across the way."

"What's Lord Mastral up to?" another cadet asked.

"He's got something planned," another one said. "He's tricky."

"Silver's breaking through!" someone else yelled.

"Going to cost them, though. There goes Silver four...and six."

The two hit craft dimmed out as the AI took over and flew them away from the battle. Asteria didn't even spare them a glance—she was staring at the wide-circling Kayser and Gull. What were they doing?

And then she saw it: they were losing altitude rapidly, dropping right down to the deck. "He's going for the river," she said.

The virtual map showed the broad break in the jungle canopy formed by the winding river course. Sure enough, both Kayser and Gull dropped down.

"They can't be more than a meter above the water," someone said. "That's crazy. They could smash."

The silvery arrows were streaks now, racing along, following the course of the river—which would bring them to within a kilometer or two of the yellow target. The remaining Silver ships had broken into individual fights with Indigo counterparts now, still fifty kilometers short of the goal. The Indigo ships were winning; they outnumbered the surviving Silver craft by a margin of three or four.

"Kayser's going to get through!" Dai cried.

The streaking Silver craft soared out of the river channel, pulled a hard right, and bore in on the target. The four defending Indigo ships had climbed to a high altitude—to try to glimpse the far-off fight, Asteria guessed. One of the defending pilots, Indigo twenty, finally spied the intruders and yelped a warning.

But too late. Gull swept in first, firing at the target. The AI reported damage: 40 percent. Fifty. Fifty-five. Then Gull had flashed past the beacon, and two of the furious Indigo pilots peeled off to blast him, which they did without much trouble.

The other two could not get within range of Kayser in time. He was at maximum speed, and he fired his weapons even before he could possibly have locked on target. He was either good or lucky, because the AI began registering hits: the target was down by fifty-seven percent, sixty, sixty-five, seventy-five, ninety…destroyed. The cadets whooped in surprise and admiration.

Dai gave Asteria a rolling-eyed look of disgust. "He couldn't have scored hits from that far out. Kayser cheated somehow."

"Sometimes you get lucky," Asteria said, but privately she suspected that Dai was right.

* * *

Both the Bolts and the Freaks survived the next day's War Games and were slated to play against each other on the third day. Team Silver also hung in, scheduled to play Team Purple. Before they met up for their briefings, Dai saw Asteria briefly. "Don't kill me if you can help it," he said with a grin. "And listen: whoever wins today, we have to kick some Aristo tail tomorrow, right?"

"Right," agreed Asteria. She was keyed up, but as it turned out the games weren't much of a challenge: Gold and Red teams were to seek each other out with long-range sensors blinded, and fight a battle of attrition. The last team to have at least one flyable ship would be the winner. Helene rose as soon as the rules had been explained and said, "Okay, let's go. I want a modified V spread. Locke, take port edge, and Meddows, be her wingman; I'll take the starboard edge, and I want Wian as wingman. Fedders, you're point..." She went on to specify their positions. They would fly in a wedge formation, with the center ships more widely spaced, the ones toward either side tightening the distance. That would allow some concentration of fire if they should happen across the enemy suddenly.

Asteria and the others didn't know anything about Team Red's formation, just that they were hunting Dai and the other Freaks over a vast square with sides a thousand kilometers long. With their long-range sensors inactive, they could detect them only from about thirty to forty klicks away. They took to the air, formed up, reached the battle area, and followed Helene's directions. They were going to cut the square on the diagonal, with everyone, but particularly those on either end of the line, straining to spot the enemy formation.

All at once, someone said, "This is Gold seven. They're behind us!"

"I see them," Helene snapped. "Coming in fast. Break apart, choose your opponent, and engage!"

Asteria looped her ship around, rolling as she came up on the outside of the formation, and then sped back along the same track she had been following. The Reds were there, five thousand meters higher than the Gold squadron, but so far they had not spotted the attackers. "I've got Red one," Asteria said as the others called their targets. The Red pilots rolled out of formation, diving to meet the challengers. Asteria fired, rolled, half-looped again. Under the rules of the game, the teams could not hear each other's communications. When Asteria zipped past a red ship, though, her enhanced senses registered the number on the fuselage: six. That was Dai.

He was good, and he had already warped into a tight turn to bring his weapons to bear on her—though she doubted he had any idea that she was his target. To him, she was an enemy ship—that was all.

She pulled up steeply and circled over into a loop. He stuck behind her, but their speed was too high for him to target accurately. Dai's lasers couldn't find her. At the crest of the loop, Asteria reversed her thrust, feeling an intense build of G forces as her ship decelerated.

Caught off-guard, Dai flashed past her, and she immediately resumed thrust. Now she was behind him; *he* had become the target. He began a series of over-and-over rolls, making it all but impossible to lock in on him. But not for Asteria, not when she was wearing her belt. In her sights, the Red ship seemed to move slowly, almost gracefully.

"Sorry, Dai," she murmured. Then she blasted him.

Two quick shots. The AI called, "Red six out!"—and Asteria went into a power dive and locked onto Red eight which was pursuing Helene.

Then she was hit, her ship judged disabled, and she relaxed as the autopilot flew her back to the hangar. She listened to the short remnant of the battle. At the end, Gold had five remaining ships; the Red squadron had been wiped out.

After the debriefing, a mock-angry Dai confronted her in the hall. "You weren't supposed to *kill* me," he said, unable to suppress a grin.

127

"I tried to bring you down with major damages," Asteria said innocently. "But I guess my concentration slipped. I—"

They turned a corner and almost collided with a man in the uniform of a commander. "A. F. Locke?" he asked.

"I—yes, that's me," Asteria said. The man's face looked grim. She had a sinking feeling that nothing good was going to come out of his mouth.

He handed her a dataslip. "Report to Vice Admiral Chen's office to answer charges," he said. "On the double."

* * *

Asteria stood at stiff attention before the Vice Admiral's desk. A stern-looking man in his forties stood beside Chen. He had frosty blue eyes and wore the uniform of a rear admiral. He did not introduce himself, nor did Chen immediately mention him. "Congratulations on your successes in the games," she said perfunctorily.

"Thank you, Commandant," Asteria replied.

She glanced at the visiting rear admiral and then said, "Locke, you are a legacy cadet, are you not?"

Why was Chen asking her that? She knew all about Asteria's father. "Yes, I am, Commandant," she said. "My father was an Academy graduate. A warrant officer."

"Who served aboard the *Adastra*," Chen added.

"Yes, Commandant. That's right."

Chen swiveled in her chair. "Admiral Vodros, do you wish to withdraw the charge?"

"I do not!" the man snapped, his voice rough and angry. "The girl is here under false pretenses."

Asteria felt cold. The man's eyes held no hint of compassion. "Commandant?" Asteria said softly to Vice Admiral Chen. "I don't understand."

"This is Rear Admiral Earl Vodros," Chen said. "He holds that the appointment under which you were admitted was intended for your cousin, Andre Locke, not for you."

"Sir," Asteria said, "my cousin is dead."

"You admit it, then," Vodros said, his eyes steady as lasers.

Vice Admiral Chen tapped her desk as if to gain their attention. She said to Vodros—but Asteria had the sense the words were for her benefit—"Admiral, it has been a long-standing Academy policy to accept the sons or daughters of any crew-member who was aboard the *Adastra*. If you press the court-martial, I doubt very much that your charges will be upheld. Why not—"

"I stand on the code of military law," Vodros said.

"Then let's convene the panel immediately—"

"I will not be able to testify today," he interrupted coldly. "Tomorrow. At 1600 hours."

Chen said, "Very well, sir. Midshipman Locke, a court-martial has been called to look into your credentials and qualifications. You are confined to quarters until 1600 hours tomorrow. You may take your meals in the mess hall as usual."

Vodros cut in harshly, "Is she to be guarded?"

"Is there need of a guard, Midshipman?"

Asteria wondered if the pounding of her heart was audible to the two officers. "No, Commandant," she said.

"Dismissed. Go straight to your barracks, Locke."

"Aye."

129

She did an about-face and marched out, keeping her back straight. Inside she felt an almost physical pain.

She would not be able to fly in the match-up with Team Silver. Helene would be frantic.

Why did this have to happen? And why today of all days, after she had just proved herself in mock battle?

ELEVEN

I'll tell you why," Dai growled that evening as they walked back toward the barracks from the mess hall, his voice low but rough with anger. "It's very simple, really. The Earl Vodros is Yalas Kayser. Lord Mastral's uncle."

Asteria looked sideways at Dai. He stared straight ahead, his jaw clenched and his face angry. She touched his arm. "He's having me court-martialed so I can't fly against Kayser?"

Dai nodded sharply. "I told you about that family. Tricky." He took a deep breath and let it out in an exasperated sigh. "Don't worry, you're safe from washing out. The officers who serve as judges will be instructors, and everyone at the Academy knows about the *Adastra* rule."

"I'm not so sure about being safe," Asteria said gloomily. "Vodros seemed to think he had me."

Dai snorted. "If they refused you, they'd have to review the appointments of about a hundred others, half of them Aristos. It'll never happen. But what is Helene going to do? Field just twenty-four pilots?"

"No," Asteria said. "I read up on the rules for the War Games, and there's a way out. Come on, let's find her."

They located her in the common room, looking haggard and studying a tactics pulsebook. She laughed when Asteria told her she wouldn't be able to fly against Team Silver because she was facing a court-martial. "Come on," she said, her expression knowing. "You can't haze me."

"It's not a joke. It's true," Asteria said. "But you still have time—"

"You're serious, aren't you?" interrupted Helene.

"Yes! But it's not my—"

"What rule did you break to get tossed off the team?" Helene cried angrily. "You're the best pilot on the team, and without you, they'll smash us!"

"Listen," Asteria said, trying to remain calm. "I learned there's a provision for subs if there's an injury or unavoidable absence. It's okay. You can still have a full team. You can take Dai."

Helene frowned at him. "He's not as good as you."

"Thank you for your support," Dai said dryly. "Hey, find someone better. An Aristo, maybe."

Helen's face darkened. "It's not a class issue. I can't find someone good enough, not with this short notice. Maybe we could petition to have the court-martial delayed—

Asteria's face flushed. All at once she felt embarrassed. Here she was, costing her team the victory.

"Yeah, good luck with that." Dai said. "Oh, by the way, you might want to know that Rear Admiral the Earl Vodros himself is pressing the charges," he added, his voice dripping with sarcasm.

Helene turned pale. "He—he's—"

"I know who he is," Asteria said doggedly. "Look, take Dai. He's as good a pilot as I am, and he's studied Kayser's—I mean Lord Mastral's moves."

"Well…you *are* both Commoners," Helene said.

"I thought this wasn't about class. And that doesn't count in battle," Dai said, his own face turning red. "If anything, it gives me more reason to want to take him out."

"I didn't mean it that way. I guess it makes sense for a Commoner to replace a Commoner. All right, Dai, I'll transmit the request to the referees. If they approve, you're on the team. I was making Asteria Gold two for tomorrow, so that's your spot, second in command." She didn't look happy.

"Thanks," Dai said.

"Don't thank me; just don't foul up," snarled Helene. "Let's get the request in now." She sat at an AI unit and quickly entered the information. It took all of five minutes for the War Games administrator to transmit an approval back.

Asteria sighed. "That's that. I'd better get to my quarters. If they check my locater, I'd better be where they sent me." She walked toward the women's wing, and Dai walked with her as far as the door. He delayed her there for a moment, looking awkward and embarrassed.

"If you're going to wish me good night, be quick about it. I don't want to be expelled for disobeying orders," she said.

"Thanks," Dai blurted out. "For the good wishes and for telling Helene the lie about my being as good as you are."

"Just knock Kayser down tomorrow," Asteria replied coldly. "Then thank me."

* * *

Confinement to quarters meant that Asteria couldn't even watch the last mock battle in the holoroom. At breakfast, she saw Bren, but she was forbidden to speak to anyone. Still, as they left the dining hall, Bren walked past and murmured, "Going to watch the games. Hope your hearing goes well." As a med services cadet, Bren was among the thousands of students who didn't take flight training. For the first time, Asteria almost envied her. Now Bren was with the other spectators down in the common room of Bronze I, following the games on the big holovision set. Asteria could hear muffled shouts and cheers as she nervously paced her room—it was so small that pacing was more like spinning in place—fighting to contain her dull anger. At one point, she tried to call Bren and ask her what was happening only to find that she had no reception. On top of everything else, the Academy AI had overridden and disabled her transceiver, as well.

Lunchtime came—but the battle was running long, and Asteria was almost the only cadet in the mess hall. A Cybot directed her to Exile's Corner, the widely spaced round tables for one meant for those undergoing the humiliating punishment of confinement. As she jogged back to the barracks, she heard the uproar of cheers and groans from the holoroom, but she couldn't make out what had happened or who had won.

At 1600, dressed in her class A uniform, a nervous Asteria presented herself in Vice Admiral Chen's office. The administrator led her to a conference room. "Sit there," Chen said, gesturing toward a chair a few steps away from a long polished table. It looked like pimina wood, with a rich reddish-brown glow. Asteria guessed the conference room was intended for the high brass who occasionally visited the Academy. Green-shaded lamps provided soft light. Two officers already sat at the table, and a Cybot stood behind them.

"I will chair the panel," Chen said, sitting down between the other two officers. "And these will be the judges. I'll introduce you."

Asteria studied the judges as Chen named them. One, a muscular man of forty-five or so, with graying brown hair, was a Commander Havers, a political science instructor; the other was a somewhat younger woman with a shaved head, Lieutenant Commander Wardley, who taught mathematics. Neither had ever taught Asteria.

"You don't know each other," Vice Admiral Chen said, as if reading Asteria's thoughts, "so you are assured of an impartial hearing. Rear Admiral Vodros will present the prosecution's case." The commandant glanced at the clock. "He should be here now."

They waited in silence as five minutes crept slowly by. Asteria sat rigidly in her chair, trying not to fidget. Commander Havers impatiently drummed his fingers on the table, and Lieutenant Commander Wardley sat with her arms crossed. Finally, Havers said, "Vice Admiral Chen, I suggest we call the Earl and learn how much later we have to wait for him to prosecute this case."

"I concur." With a sigh, Vice Admiral Chen turned to the Cybot. "Locate Rear Admiral Vodros. Establish a communications link."

"Yes, sir." The Cybot stood in silence for another minute or so and then said, "Admiral Vodros, Vice Admiral Chen."

"My Lord Vodros," said Chen. "We are waiting for you in Conference Hall One."

"Oh, the court-martial." It was strange to hear Vodros' bored-sounding voice coming from the Cybot. "I looked into that and have decided against proceeding. It's irregular, but the cadet does fall under the *Adastra* rule, even though she isn't one of us. At any rate, I have decided there's no use in challenging a long-standing tradition. I therefore recommend the charges be dropped. But keep an eye on that Commoner."

"What?" Asteria could not suppress the angry word.

Chen's eyes flashed a warning. "We will take that under advisement, my lord. Chen out. Break the link, Cybot."

"It is done."

"He didn't even mean to prosecute!" Asteria said, leaping up from her chair and clenching her hands. "He just wanted to keep me out of the War Games!"

Chen ignored her and glanced left and right at her two fellow judges. "I suggest that the panel accept Rear Admiral Vodros' recommendation and drop all charges. Discussion? No? Then what is your pleasure?"

Commander Havers said, "I concur with the Admiral."

"And I concur as well," added Lieutenant Commander Wardley.

"So ordered," said Chen. "The Cybot will so note in the record of the proceedings. The court stands in adjournment. You remain, Cadet."

The two officers left. Asteria stood breathing hard. "It wasn't fair," she complained as soon as they were alone.

"Life is frequently unfair," Chen said. "Midshipman Locke, I give you a direct order. You are to take no action against Kain Kayser, Lord Mastral. If you do, I will personally see to your punishment. No, not another word. Your restriction to quarters is over. You are restored to good standing and all privileges. Dismissed."

"Please, Vice Admiral—"

"No discussion, Cadet. You are dismissed."

"Aye, Commandant." She did an about-face and strode out, boiling.

* * *

The barracks common room had been decorated for a party, but it was long over. A group of Commoners were taking down the streamers and cleaning the floor. Bren looked up, grinning. "Aster! Isn't it great?"

"What do you mean?" Asteria asked.

"Gold won!" Bren crowed. "By one ship! It was—oh, I forgot!"

"I'll help you," Asteria said.

One of the Commoner boys looked down from a ladder. "You don't have to do that."

"We're all Commoners together, right?" Asteria said grimly. *Right.* She glanced around. Every Commoner in Bronze 1 except Dai Tamlin was cleaning the area. She hauled over a trash bin and held a dustpan as a girl named Caytla swept confetti into it. "How did Dai do in the game?" she asked.

Bren sighed sadly. "He died."

"Too bad." Then it sank in, and Asteria looked sharply up. "You don't mean he really—"

"No," one of the guys called down. "Not really. He was going to help us, but we gave him the time off because of his heroism."

Another guy chimed in, "See, the Gold team was protecting a refugee ship, and Silver was attacking. That Mastral—"

Bren swept the projection screen of the holovision clear of confetti. "Let's show her," she said. "Replay today's War Game."

The holoprojector came to life and created a representation

of the jungle. A yellow blob represented the target, and all around it glittered the gold darts of the training ships.

The boy jumped down from his ladder and pointed. "There come the Daggers, see?"

Asteria glanced at them and then looked back at the Bolt ships, still in formation. "Which one's Dai?"

Bren pointed. "Right there, second from the lead to starboard."

"Here comes the first attack. Okay, see, the Silvers are diving from about five thousand meters...and Helene sends six Golds up...the Silvers break off..."

The miniature replay showed six Gold ships rising to pursue the nine Daggers. The skirmish didn't take long and ended with minor damage to both sides, no kills.

Asteria's breath tightened. Twelve more Silver ships were streaking in from behind. Didn't anyone see them? She felt the belt tingle, sending a surge into her system.

"Come on, come on," she growled.

"Rear guard sees them...now! Listen to Helene!"

Helene's recorded orders barked out of the speaker: "Patrol team, dive on attackers coming in from 178! Gold nineteen through twenty-four, help them! Keep tight, twenty-five!"

The six ships peeled away from formation as the six patrolling ships streaked down from the heights. Asteria felt herself willing the ships to *fire, fire, fire*—

The attackers scrambled into a disordered cloud. The calm voice of a Cybot listed the casualties: *Silver three destroyed. Silver five, 85 percent damage, weapons inoperative. Gold twenty-four destroyed. Silver nine destroyed. Silver eleven targeting, navigation disabled. Gold twenty, 15 percent damage*—

Asteria felt her heart pounding. If she'd been there...if Kayser had played fair—

The Gold team broke the Dagger attack, and of the twelve ships, ten survived to rejoin the guard formation. Silver had lost a total of eleven ships destroyed or badly damaged. Another feint from above, and this time Gold lost five ships to Silver's four. Another attack. Helene was left, along with Dai and five more Gold ships. The Daggers were down to just six—and three of those had not yet showed up. Silver one had been conspicuously absent.

Helene redeployed the guards, using what she had. The refugee ship was almost to its landing site—if they could bring it in, Gold would win—

"Endgame," Bren said. "Here they come."

Four of the surviving Daggers were circling the landing site. They sped directly toward the approaching target ship, and the Gold team tightened formation to meet them.

"There's Kayser!" Asteria said.

He was using the same trick he had used earlier. He and his wingman were on the same heading as the Gold team but so low they were hard to see. As the target and the Gold team roared overhead, Silver one and two tilted up and stabbed through the air, directly at the target ship—

"Daggers below!" Dai's voice. Gold two dived and circled. A moment later, Helene followed him, but they were going to be too late—

Kayser's weapons fired. Dai rolled his ship, dropped, and took the brunt of the fire. The Cybot announced, "Gold two destroyed."

But Helene was firing. "Silver one destroyed. Silver two disabled—"

"Foul," Kayser's angry voice spat. "Foul!"

The Cybot announced the destruction or disabling of almost every Silver and Gold ship, one by one...until only Helene was left, limping along with 53 percent damage. "The decision is in favor of the Gold team," the Cybot announced. "The Gold team wins the exercise."

The cadets in the common room raised a cheer, startling Asteria.

"Dai saved the day," Bren said.

"Yeah," agreed Asteria. "But if I'd been there—" She tried to force herself to relax. "Yeah," she said again. "He did. Good for Dai."

But she felt cheated all the same.

"The win hasn't been confirmed yet," warned the Commoner boy, climbing back on his ladder. "Because Lord Mastral's lodged a formal complaint that he was fouled."

"It won't stick," Bren told Asteria. "The AI agrees with the referees that Gold won." She dropped her voice to a confidential tone. "But now Lord Mastral will have it in for Dai."

"Dai will have to join the club," Asteria said, dumping colorful confetti into the waste bin.

twelve

ater that same evening she found an exhausted Dai slumped on a bench in the courtyard of the Bronze Barracks. No one else was there. The soft spring dusk was coming on, and Asteria let herself sink onto the bench beside him, inhaling the minty air—the early pale-pink versilla blooms in the flower beds were waving in the evening breeze. The central fountain sent up a graceful, silvery plume of water that swayed gently with the light wind. Dai grunted an almost inaudible greeting and put his arm on the back of the bench behind her.

Asteria let herself lean back against it, amused by Dai's shy physical gesture. "Heard you did well today," she said.

He turned and stared at her profile. "How did the court-martial go?" he asked anxiously.

"It didn't." She explained what had happened in a few bitter words.

"See?" demanded Dai, his tone tight. "This is corruption, that's what it is. The Fleet is supposed to be better than that! Vodros stepped in to protect wittle Mastral, that's all. He never intended to push the trial through—he just wanted you off the opposing team."

Asteria reminded him: "It didn't work, though. You were there instead of me."

He moved his arm from behind her and leaned forward, tensely, as if he were angry with himself or with the world in general. "Yeah. I got killed."

"I heard about it. But it was a tactical decision, right? You sacrificed your ship to save the target, and that won the game for the Gold team."

Dai sounded frustrated when he said, "I had to run flat-out just ahead of Mastral. Couldn't turn, couldn't do anything but take his fire. I wish I could have brought my weapons to bear. I didn't even get in one shot—just caught all of Mastral's lasers. The only thing that I accomplished was to buy Helene enough time to get into firing position and bring the little snot down." Dai balled his fist and struck his knee. "But calling a court-martial just to throw you off the team—that's not right. Vodros is a rear admiral! He has no business trying to futz around in Academy business while the Tetras are attacking again."

"What?" Asteria blinked. Overhead, the intense stars of the Corona cluster were already gleaming in the purple sky. "Where are they attacking?"

"Peshwan outposts," Dai said. "I guess you didn't hear. The news came in today. It wasn't a major Tetra force. Just a few dozen probes, but they destroyed a relay station and took out five drone ships before a Fleet Dreadnaught wiped them up. The *Victory,* crew complement of two hundred, weaponry—"

"I know the specs," Asteria said. She thought for a few moments and added, "I wonder what the Tetras are like. Physically, I mean. Are they humanoid or reptilian or insectoid, or like nothing we've ever seen? And why do they attack our settlements? They don't seem to colonize the planets they conquer."

"They haven't conquered any since the First Tetra War," Dai reminded her. "And who knows what they look like? All we've ever captured have been mechanized ships with silicon AI systems—and they don't even seem to have a language. We never hear any comm chatter, and the captured Tetra ships don't have any written language anywhere in them that we can find. If we ever negotiate a peace, I don't know how we'll do it."

"We don't have an actual Tetra body, but we've found tissue," Asteria pointed out.

"Yeah, one time, and even that wasn't certain. It was tetraploid tissue, but it might not have been from a pilot—could have been a specimen of some alien animal that ship had collected. There wasn't enough left to reconstruct a body configuration."

Crees were beginning to hum in the bushes. Asteria reflected that she had never seen a cree, either: small insects native to Dromia that didn't bite or sting but were known only for their gentle, musical droning sounds. She looked up at the sky. The brilliant, tiny orb of Coriam shone like a sapphire halfway up the sky to the north, above the flat roof of the mess hall. She wondered, not for the first time, what life on the privileged world of the Aristos must be like.

She took in a deep breath, smelling the minty aroma of the blossoms, which seemed to be growing more intense as the evening drew on. The crees murmured. It all seemed so peaceful. "Well, we won't have to worry about Tetra attacks here," Asteria said. "I just wanted to congratulate you for winning the battle."

"Thanks."

"Well, are you going to tell me about it?"

"It was close," Dai said grudgingly. "Did they tell you we won by one ship, and that one was within seven points of exploding?"

"I heard."

"Well, this is how it happened." Slowly at first, and then with a growing intensity, Dai went over the whole battle: the arrangement of the two teams, the mass attack that he recognized as a feint—it was the same basic battle plan that Kayser had used once before. "I checked the map to see how Kayser planned to sneak up on the refugee ship. Same skimmer they'd used before, by the way. Anyhow, no rivers, no canyons, but there was one point where we were sailing along above the western cliffs, and I figured he'd drop down almost to sea level and follow the coastline."

Dai picked up a twig and bent down to sketch in the dirt. "Here's where the skimmer would pass over the cliffs. It's only a few kilometers up to where we turned inland again, so I thought if Mastral was going to try to sneak-attack us, this would be the place. I told Helene what I thought would happen, and she had me go up to 2,500 and hang back. Sure enough when Gull and Mastral came swooping up for the attack, I saw them in plenty of time to dive. I called Helene..." He tossed the twig aside. "You know the rest of it. I didn't have much to do with the actual win, because I had no way of working into firing position. Just a matter of getting in front of Mastral and not letting him get a clear shot at the skimmer."

"You were brilliant," Asteria said. "It was the only way to deal with that kind of an attack."

"It worked, anyway. We won."

"Congratulations. I'm sorry I missed the party."

"Yeah, me too. Gold Team would never have been in the running if it hadn't been for your victories earlier. And congratulations to you, too, on escaping from Vodros' clutches," Dai said. He leaned back and stared up at Coriam, as if gazing in scorn on all Aristos everywhere. "I know one thing for certain. If I ever get to be commander in chief, the first general order I'm going to issue is that in the Royal Space Fleet, there will be no further discrimination against Commoners."

"They won't let a Commoner become commander in chief," Asteria reminded him.

"See what I mean?" wailed Dai, spreading his arms to the sky, as though imploring the stars. "Discrimination!"

* * *

The next twelve days passed rapidly, a welcome break in the routine of the Academy. The whole school hung on the War Games, tension building with each round. The second-year teams faced more intricate tactical situations than the first-year teams had confronted; the third-years were able to use more advanced simulated weapons and larger training craft, and the fourth-years actually got to fight in space. The senior class cadets did not fly in single-pilot craft like the first-years, or small strike vessels with crews of six like second-years, or even destroyers like the third-years—but in full battleships, each with a crew of twenty-five to thirty.

It was true that the battleships were only simulators—a real cruiser would have a crew of a hundred or more, not just twenty-five cadets and a gaggle of Cybots, each Cybot taking the place of twenty humans. Still, the ships were almost full-sized, and on the holos, their maneuvers and firepower were almost as impressive. Watching them, Asteria yearned to be at the controls of one of those big warbirds—or better, handling a real one. Going against real enemies. Against Tetras.

Against Raiders. Against those who had destroyed her family.

The fourth-year victors were Team Galaxy. They successfully defended an asteroid (standing in for an outpost planet) against a deadly wave of simulated Tetra needle-ships—larger than life-sized, because a human could not fit in one of the tiny Tetra craft. The Academy gave the cadets one whole day of celebration—and the very next day, it was back to the grind.

In the meantime, Asteria became keenly aware that Kain Kayser was a smoldering volcano waiting to erupt. When his claim of having been fouled was summarily rejected by the judges—even after his uncle had demanded a reconsideration of the judgment—Kayser clearly had developed a brand-new grudge against Dai. And just as clearly, he still nurtured the old one against Asteria, ignoring the uneasy truce he had agreed to. In the common room one evening, he loudly argued with his cronies that Commoners should not even be permitted to enroll at the Academy.

"Their brains aren't developed," he had said. "They don't have the capacity to absorb and retain information that an Aristocrat does. Oh, I'll grant you they have a kind of animal cunning. They can do things like trick their way into the Academy when they don't have any right to be here."

"They can also beat you at piloting," Helene called across the room.

Kayser gave her a sour look. "You're an Aristocrat, though a low-ranking one, and you were the one who shot me down," he said. "The Commoner just got in my way, that's all. Anyway, I hear that the results of the War Games might not count. An admiral is looking into an irregular substitution. The whole last game probably will be voided."

"What admiral is it? Your uncle?" Asteria asked him.

Kayser ignored her and turned back to his friends, dropping his voice and muttering. But they looked at her and laughed nastily.

Don't let yourself get mad, Asteria told herself. *Another few weeks, final examinations, and then you're in space for the whole summer. Don't risk it. Don't get mad.*

Because she had a secret to protect. If she could manage it, her summer in space wouldn't just be a round of observing. She would somehow get into a real fighting ship. And then—

She imagined a Raider ship in her sights: not just any ship, but the one she had seen leaving the shattered agridome. The one that had carried the ones who had killed her cousin and her father. She itched to open fire—

No. Best not to think about it yet. Later, there would be time. But she had to make sure that she did nothing that might disqualify her from summer space duty.

Still, it was getting harder and harder to control her temper. She kept a lid on it with difficulty, but the pressure built up. It drove her to push herself even harder. Physically, she was in the best shape of her life, bench-pressing fifty-six Standard kilos, able to run eight kilometers without pausing, knocking down top marks in every PT test. With Dai's help, she struggled through chemistry. She slowly managed to improve, notching her first 3.0 grades in the last part of spring term. Her overall

147

average crept up too; sheer stubbornness prevented her from scoring anything lower than a three. She and Kayser were tied at 3.6. It wasn't the highest average in the class—at least half a dozen others had better ones—but she didn't care about being first, just about being better than Kayser.

Her best class was flight training. She had a 3.9 there, while Kayser was stuck at 3.7. He complained constantly about not being treated fairly—though Dai maintained that the flight instructors always bent the rules for him—and insisted on three tries before finally conceding that he could not match Asteria's time in a speed trial. Still, he claimed that the fault was mechanical; his trainer, he said, had a defective drive.

That should have been a triumph for Asteria, but all the effort she was putting into classes was wearing her down. She always felt starved for sleep, and the bad temper that she kept from showing around Kayser seemed to bubble up in other ways.

One evening as five of the Bronze 1 Commoners were reviewing for a chem exam, Dai patiently explained—for the third time—covalent bonding.

"I still don't understand the concept," Asteria said.

Bren leaned forward. "It's a negative-to-positive stable attraction—"

"I didn't ask you!" snapped Asteria. "Dai's the one with the 4.0 chem average!"

Bren flinched. "Sorry."

Dai quickly tried to smooth things over: "I guess I'm better at understanding it than explaining it. Okay, Bren's right about the stability."

Asteria felt a dull ache. The pain in Bren's eyes hurt her too. Asteria was too ashamed of herself even to apologize. And then at the next midbreak, while she and Dai were playing an informal game of netball, she scored two points in quick succession and lashed out at Dai for laughing about it.

"You're losing!" she reminded him, throwing her racquet down.

"Hey, it's only a game!" he protested.

She stamped her foot. "If you don't take it seriously, what's the point of even playing?"

He shot back, "If you take it all that seriously, it stops being a game. Come on, Aster, I'm not Mastral."

"Sorry," she said grudgingly. She bent over to pick up her racquet. "Go ahead, serve."

Added to her stress was a worry that she shared with no one: The belt around her waist was...different. It had been made of flat links; somehow the metal had *flowed together,* and now it was a smooth but flexible band around her stomach, four inches wide. And it felt different too: still tough and resistant, but somehow pliant, as if it were alive. She dreamed about it some nights, dreamed that it spoke to her. Or questioned her: "What do you need?"

What in the universe had Carlson Locke stored away? Alien tech, someone had suggested. Was the belt something made by the Tetras? Was it dangerous?

Was it changing?

Was it changing *her?*

At times, she would have sworn that it was. Especially when she was encased in the trainer, executing a tricky maneuver or straining for speed. She could *feel* energy surging in the belt, shooting into her when she needed an extra edge, faster reflexes, and a burst of strength. Nobody could touch her in the physical defense classes now—she held the champion slot and had a perfect score, 4.0, in hand-to-hand. When an attacker came toward her, she had the oddest sensation of entering some physical zone that was far removed from everyday life. She perceived the opponent as moving in slow motion, at half speed. She had all the time she needed to ward off a blow, catch the opponent off-balance, and get through his or her defenses.

And she thought all those...advantages...were streaming from the belt. As if it plugged into her nervous and muscular systems, the way she plugged into the trainer, and boosted her abilities.

Afterward, she was always ravenously hungry. The meals in the mess hall had not improved, but she wolfed down the bland, tasteless food nevertheless. When her weight began to fall, the Cybots in charge of the mess hall started giving her a little extra at each meal—Dai claimed they were punishing her—and she had to report to sick bay for a metabolism analysis. Still, the medical Cybot could find nothing wrong with her except that she was revved a little higher than most girls her age. Vitamins and a slightly increased food ration were the only treatments it prescribed.

Somehow, she held it all together for several weeks. But she had the feeling that if Kayser didn't let up in his constant hectoring and harassment, one day she would lose it.

thirteen

ocke," the PT instructor said, "partner with Lord Mastral."
"Are you kidding?" Kayser spat, scowling.

The self-defense class was being held outside; the day was unseasonably warm. They were playing a game of capture the beacon. Not only did the two opposing sides have to fight each other individually in hand-to-hand combat, but they had to work as teams—each team trying to defend its own flashing beacon and prevent the other team from switching it off.

"My lord," the instructor said calmly, "you haven't faced her all term. You must have a designated opponent—"

"I've hurt my ankle," Kayser claimed in an annoyed voice. "Disaster has a grudge against me. Everyone knows that. I can't fight her with my weak ankle. She'd deliberately try to injure me."

The instructor looked at him with no expression. "I received no notification of your injury from the med staff, my lord. But I will take your word for it. Very well. You can sit out—"

"No, I want to play. Because I can't run, I'll be the goal defender instead," Kayser said. "You'll have to let me use a borral stick, though. Because of my ankle."

"No fair!" Santos Markand, the beacon guard on Asteria's side, objected. "If he gets to use a borral, I do too!" Borral sticks were long, double-headed clubs, the heads padded. They were never used in unarmed combat practice.

"There will be no weapons," the instructor said firmly. "The rules of this game allow open-hand combat only. Very well, my lord, you may defend your side's beacon. Vanyon, switch places with Count Mastral and partner with Locke. Everyone set? Good. Onto your own side of the field and take your starting positions. At my signal. Ready?" He whistled shrilly, and the two sides clashed in the middle of the field.

Asteria had fought Vanyon before, a slim guy who did not flaunt his Aristo background—and who had a healthy respect for Asteria's speed and strength. Vanyon didn't press an attack, and he didn't defend with much enthusiasm, though he blocked and delayed her when she tried to break away to reach the other side's goal. Vanyon clearly wasn't interested in a real fight, just in a stalemate of dodging and weaving.

Very well, Asteria decided. She would accommodate him. She led him halfway around the field, picking up the pace. Vanyon tired before she did. Choosing her moment, Asteria faked him out of position, broke for the enemy beacon, and weaved her way through fighting pairs. Vanyon ran after her, too slow to catch up. Moving in front of the goal to block her, Kayser screamed, "You idiot! Stop her! Don't let her get through!"

Vanyon desperately threw himself forward and grabbed her ankle, tripping her. As she toppled forward, Asteria tucked her shoulder in and rolled, feeling the now-familiar jolt of power from the belt, sensing the weird slowing of time. She saw and heard with a new clarity: colors and sounds were intense, distinct. It was as if her senses had been sharpened tenfold. She turned her fall into a controlled maneuver, tumbled forward, bounded up again onto her feet, and caught Vanyon with a sidelong blow, sending him sprawling. She spun to confront a white-faced Kayser. He crouched—he had learned long ago that bladehand was not a good approach against her, and he settled into a wary defensive posture.

She circled him, planning her move. The beacon, a flashing red light atop a thin mast, was within reach. Vanyon was scrambling up, now behind Kayser from her vantage point.

"Get her, stop her, help me!" Kayser growled over his shoulder.

Asteria feinted left, moved right, and almost got past Kayser—and then felt a sudden painful shock that thrummed through her whole body and made her muscles seize up momentarily. Kayser had palmed a small stunner, and he had shot her. The charge should have knocked her off her feet; but something—an adrenaline rush, the belt she wore, something—sent a wave of fierce energy through her body, and she recovered almost instantly.

In that instant, she forgot about the beacon. Lumbering, panting, Vanyon charged in, and she used a hasty pivot throw to put him down. This time, he landed on his back so hard that the breath chuffed out of him. He did not look as though he were in a hurry to rise again.

Everything was moving so slowly. *Stop it, stop it,* Asteria told herself. *It's just a game. He's not a real threat!*

But she felt as if she were about to lose control. Under her singlet, a strange sensation crept all along her torso. Then Kayser lunged forward and shot her again in the solar plexus—but the belt had *grown* beneath her singlet and now covered her skin right up to the neck. Somehow it absorbed the energy beam, and she barely felt it, just a mild tingling. *Don't hurt him. Don't!* she warned herself as she darted toward Kayser.

"My ankle!" Kayser yelped, leaping back as she moved toward him. He raised the stunner, but it had not recharged.

Asteria waded in past his defenses, seized his wrist, spun him, and twisted until he dropped the weapon. He writhed in her grasp, screaming, "Foul! Foul! She's hurting my ankle!"

Another opponent tried to intervene. With her free hand, Asteria blocked the attacker's two blows, and then she delivered a sudden thrust that took the wind out of him. She let go of Kayser's wrist, and when he tried to stumble away from her, she seized him and used his momentum to throw him facedown in the grass. He skidded on his stomach, yelping in surprise and outrage. She reached up, switched off the beacon—

The world returned to normal. She heard for the first time the angry shrieking blasts of the instructor's whistle.

Her side was cheering.

Kayser rolled over and lay on his side, holding his ankle and groaning piteously. Asteria looked for the stunner he had smuggled into the game and didn't see it, but Gull was standing in the general area where it had been dropped.

"Get up, my lord," the instructor said, coming toward them, his expression serious. "Walk it off."

"She tried to break my weak ankle!" shouted Kayser, pointing at Asteria with a shaking finger. "She's a Commoner! They're not supposed to lay hands on us!"

"There's an exception for physical training," the instructor said, crouching beside him. He said dryly, "With your permission,

FLIGHT OF THE OUTCAST

my lord." Then he gingerly felt Kayser's ankle. The fallen cadet whimpered as he did so. "No broken bones that I can feel, but if it hurts that badly, let's make sure. Gull, help Lord Mastral to sick bay to have his ankle checked. Locke, you could have moved past him without that last throw. Take a demerit."

"No," she said. "He cheated. He had a weapon."

"She's lying!" Kayser shouted. "The lying little—"

"Silence!" roared the instructor. "Can anyone verify that? Who was closest?"

"I, uh, I didn't see a weapon," Vanyon said hastily.

"It was a mini stunner," Asteria said. "He shot me twice."

"If I'd done that, she wouldn't be standing," Kayser insisted. "*She* broke the rules, not me!"

"He has a point, Locke," the instructor said. "No one could take two close-range stunner hits and stay on her feet. Don't argue with me. Congratulations on your win, but the demerit stays. You're finished for the day. Go shower. The rest of you, form up."

Alone in the echoing shower room, Asteria stripped off her PT uniform and saw that the belt had returned to normal: just a broad silver circlet, not some weird kind of beam-absorbing body armor. She stepped under the shower and lathered herself with soap. Then, fiercely, she tried to shove the belt down, over her hips, so she would be free of it. It refused to budge. She wriggled and pushed harder and didn't give up until she was panting with effort.

"All right," she muttered. "Stay there." She rinsed, dried, and got dressed, not really knowing if she were more pleased or upset that the belt was on for good.

* * *

Asteria wasn't too surprised to be summoned back to Vice Admiral Chen's office that afternoon. The Admiral said, "I have another formal complaint against you, Cadet."

"From Rear Admiral Vodros?" asked Asteria, fighting to remain composed.

"No, not this time. From Count Mastral's father, Earl Kayser. He alleges that you deliberately attacked his son, though Lord Mastral was suffering from an injury at the time. He reminds me that it is a major offense for a Commoner to strike an Aristocrat. I want to hear your side of the story. Tell me the circumstances."

Tight-lipped, Asteria told the commandant about the capture-the-beacon game, leaving out the part about the stunner—it was long gone, and she knew that any mention of it would be seen as her attempt to excuse her actions. "I didn't do anything to his ankle," she finished. "To reach the objective, I threw him facedown on the grass. It shouldn't have hurt his foot."

Vice Admiral Chen consulted her desk readout. "Sick bay says Count Mastral has no detectable damage to his ankle, but we cannot assume that an Aristocrat is lying, so there is possibly some soft-tissue injury that does not show up on imaging or medscans." She settled back in her chair and gazed at Asteria, her expression unreadable. "These are serious charges, Cadet. Earl Kayser wants you expelled."

"Commandant," Asteria said, swallowing hard, "I insist that is not fair. We were in class when it happened. I followed the instructor's orders. I played the game according to the rules."

"Did you? The instructor tells me that he can't swear that you did. He says you moved so fast you were just a blur. Are you really that good?"

"When I need to be," Asteria said. "Commandant."

Vice Admiral Chen said, "You will, I hope, be relieved to hear that in my opinion this is not a matter warranting expulsion. However, Earl Kayser is powerful on this planet. I am going to place you on behavioral warning, Cadet. Any further infractions will result in severe punishment. Your permission to leave campus on the Haven visits is rescinded for the remainder of the academic year. Now, I notice that you have applied for space duty during the off term. I'll have to reconsider that."

"Commandant?"

Patiently, the vice admiral explained, "I can't give you what amounts to a reward if your behavior is bad. I told you these are serious charges. It doesn't matter if they are true or not. You are on probation, Cadet. If you can keep yourself off report for the rest of the term—just four more weeks—then I'll allow you space duty. If not, your request for a space assignment is denied."

"But, Commandant—I don't have anywhere to go in the summer if I don't get space duty," Asteria said desperately. "I don't have a home. You know that. I can't go back to Theron. The Bourse probably would arrest me."

"If you are an outcast, Cadet Locke, it is because of your own decisions," the vice admiral said firmly. "Behave yourself from now on. And avoid Count Mastral. I don't want to hear any more complaints. Dismissed."

The long summer of Dromia was coming on, and the campus lay in stifling midday heat and humidity—especially for someone who had grown up on a cool world. Asteria's temper simmered in the sweltering air. On her way back to the barracks, she passed the eroded statue of Empyrator Kyseros, brooding on the little round stone island in the center of his circular reflecting pool. Asteria had no tokens to toss to the God of 2.5. She had no requests to address to him. But standing in the harsh sunlight, feeling the muggy air lying thick in her lungs, she made him a promise: "No Aristo is going to kick me out of the Academy. Kayser can't do it. His father can't do it—even you couldn't do it. I'm staying."

The statue gazed at her across the water and, like all statues, kept his thoughts to himself.

Asteria tried hard to keep her head down over the next few days. She forced herself to ignore Kayser and his friends. She approached classes with grim determination to study, to do well, and to avoid calling attention to herself. Bren seemed to have forgiven her for her short temper, but Bren acted subdued around her too. Asteria studied until she was exhausted, and then she fell into her cot and dreamed of cambots following her around, spying on her.

Dai looked almost as tired as Asteria felt. They still studied together, but they didn't chat much outside of their study sessions. Final exams were coming up soon, and both of them were working hard to cram their heads with information. Dai gave up his visit to Haven the next weekbreak day in favor of reviewing chemistry.

While the older students enjoyed time off, Asteria sat with Dai in the common room, working at her AI unit.

Asteria's screen suddenly froze and a banner scrolled across: *Cadet Locke, report to Commandant's office now.*

"Oh, great," groaned Asteria.

Dai glanced at the screen and frowned. "What did you do now?"

Asteria's face felt hot. "Nothing!" When he gave her a doubtful grimace, she insisted, "I mean it—I haven't done anything! I've stayed away from Kayser. I've concentrated on my studies. I've crammed for finals—that's it!"

"Well, then, good luck," Dai said quietly. "I hope Mastral's stinking family hasn't cooked something else up against you."

There was only one way to find out. Asteria double-timed to the administration building and stepped from a scorching day into the cool air-conditioning. Vice Admiral Chen saw her at once and waved her into a chair. "How are your studies going?" she asked.

"Well, thank you, Commandant. I'm hoping for a high three average."

"I see you have a perfect score in PT despite your demerits. And you seem to have quite a gift as a pilot. Concentrate on the chemistry, and you should reach your goal. I've called you here, Cadet Locke, to tell you that the matter of your father's estate has finally been resolved in your favor."

"Oh," Asteria said in surprise.

"Baron Kamedes appointed a commission that validated your father's claim to the land; the Bourse in—what is it?—Sanctal have agreed to surrender control of the estate to a conservator. Now, you can legally inherit on your sixteenth birthday. That's in—"

"Two years and ten Standard days, Commandant," murmured Asteria, feeling her stomach flutter. That meant that the anniversary of her father's death was in twenty days. She had not thought about that before.

"Study this." Chen pushed a dataslip across her desk, and Asteria picked it up. The commandant added, "I'll give you the gist of it. Your best choice, it appears to me, is to agree to resell the estate back to the local government. They will pay three hundred thousand credits for it. You will owe five thousand credits to the Bourse as local taxes and as reimbursement for their services to you following your father's death. Baron Kamedes is asserting the right to tax the estate at 50 percent. That will leave you with a hundred and forty-five thousand credits—you will be a very rich Commoner."

Asteria didn't say anything. Money wasn't what she wanted.

"However, you can make up your own mind," Vice Admiral Chen said. "Remember, though, if you decide to continue farming, you will still owe the taxes. You could choose to sell half the land to cover them—but then you would owe more taxes on the income. It's not easy to realize a full profit when you're dealing with the baron's government. If you want any advice, the Academy has counselors and legal advisors you can consult before making any decision—"

"Tell them to sell it," Asteria said, her voice shaky. "I'm not going back to live on Theron, Commandant."

The commandant nodded. "I understand. Very well, I'll have the Academy consultants put your decision into the proper form. You will have to authorize it, but that's a formality. If you return tomorrow at the same time, I think everything can be taken care of. As to your inheritance—do you have an account?"

"No, Commandant," Asteria said. "I've never had any money."

"We'll establish an account for you on Dromia. Most Fleet Officers maintain one here."

"I don't want Aristos to administer it," Asteria told her.

"The Royal Fleet is in charge of the bank, Cadet. Not the Aristocracy. Will you take my word on that?"

Asteria didn't have to think for very long. "Yes."

"Very well. We'll establish the account as soon as we can arrange for the transfer of funds. That may involve a brief trip to Theron for you, because the Bourse are very specific about the way funds transfers must be authorized."

"I...I don't want to go back there," Asteria said.

The commandant nodded. "I know you don't, but you're a cadet now—practically Empyrean property. Believe me, the Bourse would not dare to hold you. If I can, I will arrange for your summer space tour to allow you enough time at the end to fly to Theron, where you can settle everything. Now, as to the actual credits: Until you are fourth-year, there will be a limit on the withdrawals you can make, but that would hold true even if you were an Aristocrat. You will gain full control of everything upon your graduation. Is that all acceptable?" When Asteria did not immediately reply, Chen said quietly, "Do you trust me, Aster?"

Asteria took a deep breath. "Yes."

"Very well. That's all, Cadet. Dismissed."

"Thank you, Commandant."

Dai was waiting for her outside Bronze 1. "What happened?" he asked anxiously.

"I'm rich," she said flatly, and told him about it.

He whistled. "That's like ten years' salary for a fighter captain!" he exclaimed. "I don't think my whole family's worth that much. Congratulations."

She nodded, and then an involuntary sob burst from her throat.

"What's wrong?"

She shook her head. In a shaky voice, she said, "It's not right. I feel like they're trying to…to bribe me to keep quiet. Space Fleet hasn't done a thing to track down the Raiders who—who—never mind." She broke off, not wanting to cry in front of him.

"They can't do anything on their own, not in a Fringe system," Dai said in a comforting tone, falling into step beside her. "Kamedes has to formally ask for assistance."

Asteria balled her hands into tight fists. "Then why doesn't he?"

Dai shrugged. "Who knows? He's an Aristo. Maybe he's afraid of losing status by—hey, hey, I'm sorry. I didn't mean to upset you."

Asteria walked fast. A tear fell from her eye. She quickly wiped it away, breathing fiercely.

Dai trailed along behind her. "I'm sorry," he said again. "Is there anything I can do to help?"

No one could help.

No one could bring back Carlson Locke.

part 3
against the odds

FOURTEEN

Graduation day: a hot morning under a steely blue sky. Some eight thousand cadets and more than twice that many family members and friends sat in the vast Punchbowl, a dead volcanic caldera on the edge of the campus that had been made into the largest amphitheater on the planet. Dai and Asteria, as lowly first-years, sat almost as far from the stage as possible. From there, they could barely see the figures in dress uniforms. For their benefit, an enormous holoscreen hovered fifty meters in the air, and on it, they saw the speakers in close-up.

Asteria felt a bit overwhelmed. She was looking at more people than she had ever seen at one time. The cadet section was a rainbow. Up front were the graduating fourth-years, resplendent in their sky blue uniforms. Behind them sat rank on rank of third-years, a swath of navy blue. Second-years in their maroon uniforms sat just behind them, and then the first-years, all wearing the same green as Dai and Asteria, formed the last great stripe. The families on either side of the rows of cadets were splotches of all colors.

A retired admiral, a white-haired old man, was droning on: "Most of you will never see actual combat. However, that does not make your role as Fleet Officers any less vital. The Fleet has a thousand responsibilities—"

Asteria sat wishing that the planetary weather engineers had more control over temperature. They had delivered a sunny day, but the best they could do still left the air a sultry 34 degrees. In the heat, the admiral lost his place in his speech, repeated part of it, finished, sat down to loud applause, and then Vice Admiral Chen took the lectern. "Thank you, Admiral Obrey," she said with a tight smile. "And that brings us to the part of the ceremony you have all waited for. Graduating class, please stand."

They did, all 2,612 of them, with a sound like a wind rustling in the trees. The commandant said, "By the power vested in me by Space Fleet Command, I accept all of you and each of you into the Royal Space Fleet with the rank of junior lieutenant. Congratulations to you all. May your courage never fail, may your skills remain sharp, and may you always serve the Empyrator loyally. I present to you all the graduates of Empyrean Year Standard 2410."

The crowd, parents and cadets alike, roared its approval. The commandant's order of dismissal could hardly be heard, but the remaining cadets all stood, ten thousand of them, and gave the graduates one last cheer.

Dai said something Asteria couldn't hear. "What?"

"I said I hope that will be us one day!"

Only about one-sixth of any entering class ever graduated. The others would be washed out or redirected into support staff training.

Asteria swallowed. *I'll make it*, she told herself. After all, she was one of the first-years who had done well enough to be allowed to attend the graduation ceremony, and that was a minority. And she had done so well in flight training—*No,* she told herself. *Don't think about it. Don't plan too much. Just concentrate on getting through the next three years.*

They marched back to Bronze 1 in formation, answered questions from the unlucky cadets whose averages had been too low to allow them to attend the ceremony, and packed. Most of the cadets were heading home for the summer break.

Fifteen hundred were going into space. The lucky ones, Dai said, but Asteria wasn't so sure.

Asteria and Kayser had been assigned to the same ship, the *Pax*, a Sword-class cruiser, a cut above the destroyer that she and Dai had boarded to hitch a ride to Corona. Dai's orders instructed him to report for duty aboard a maintenance and repair vessel, the *Granite*. "Dull, dull, dull!" he wailed. Asteria couldn't help but feel angry...and suspicious. Angry that Dai only cared about his own excitement and not sharing the same ship with her, suspicious that she and Kayser were assigned together. Who had approved that after all of their drama? Was somebody looking to get her in trouble?

That evening, she said good-bye to Valesa, Gala, and Bren. Bren said, "Hey, don't be so gloomy. We'll be back next fall. And you're going into space!"

"I know," Asteria said, trying to smile. "But—well, I haven't always been a great friend. I'm sorry about that."

Bren gave her a quick hug. "Nobody's perfect! I can be sort of—"

"Make way!"

They all turned. Dai Tamlin was walking carefully toward them, holding a cake decorated with one candle. "I wish this were fancier," he said. "But even with all my scrounging talents and all my persuasion, this measly little thing was all I could get from the mess hall. Happy birthday, Asteria!"

Asteria's throat tightened.

"It's your birthday?" Valesa asked.

She shook her head.

Dai set the cake—chocolate, and just about the right size for five to share—down on a study desk. "Not until tomorrow," he said. "But we won't be together tomorrow, so—anyway, on Theron it may already be her birthday. Who knows?"

They all sang to her, and she tried to look pleased.

But it was the first birthday she had ever had without her father there to share it. Dai goofed and joked and served slices of the cake, and when he had a moment, he said quietly to her, "I wish I could have gotten you a present. Best I could do is to get your friends together."

"That's not true," she said. "You also got me cake."

* * *

The next morning was still clear but even hotter. Carrying her one piece of luggage, a heavy duffle, Asteria reported to the shuttle pad. She cleared her orders through a Cybot and found her place in line.

Kain Kayser was already there. She fell into place behind him. He gave her a curt nod.

The boarding door vanished, and the line of cadets trooped in. They were to sit back to back. Asteria carefully took the left turn when Kayser took the right, just so they wouldn't have to sit next to each other. The air lock began to close when a frantic voice yelped, "Wait!"

The Cybot reopened the lock, and everyone turned in their seats as a red-headed boy hurtled aboard the shuttle. "Orders were changed at the last minute!" he gasped.

"Look who's here," teased Kayser, in as easygoing a voice as Asteria had ever heard.

"Sit down," the Cybot instructed Dai.

Hastily, Dai stowed his bag in the underseat bin and slid into place in the front row, fastening the restraints. On impulse, Asteria unlatched herself and quickly moved up to take the one remaining empty seat beside him.

"What happened?" she whispered.

"*Please* secure your seat restraints," said the Cybot pilot, sounding as close to exasperation as a machine could.

Dai shrugged. "I put in a request for transfer, and Chen approved it ten minutes ago. Didn't think I'd make it—"

"You did cut it close," Kayser called from behind them, sounding amused.

"Yeah, I did," Dai muttered.

"We are ready for liftoff," the pilot announced. The ship engaged the grav drive, and as soon as it had risen a few hundred meters, it switched to ion propulsion. The cadets whooped as the G forces pressed them against their seat restraints, and the shuttle soared at full power up toward Sync-1, the station from which they would depart on the *Pax*.

Asteria looked past Dai to see the horizon of Dromia become a rounded arc, to see the blue sky darken to violet and then to star-studded blackness.

"Look, you two," Kayser muttered loudly, "about this summer—"

"What about it?" Dai asked, twisting around to frown at him.

Kayser shrugged. "We're going to be stuck on the *Pax.* We'll have to work together. Remember the truce?"

"Yes," Asteria said coldly. "That lasted a long time, didn't it?"

"My fault," Kayser said. "I didn't treat you well. I admit it. But we'll be rated on cooperation. So—can we start over? I can't control my uncle. I'm sorry he butted in, and I'm glad the court-martial didn't take place, all right? If we can't be friends, can we at least agree to be shipmates?"

Dai was gripping the arms of his seat—the shuttle had switched off its engines, and in orbit, free fall had sent them into zero G, always a queasy moment—and said, "All right with me, if you're being honest...my lord." He pronounced the last two words with extra emphasis.

Asteria bit her lip. "I won't start anything if you won't," she said.

"Agreed," Kayser said. "Hey, do you know where we're going, Di—I mean, Aster?"

Asteria shook her head. "Just that it's a patrol vessel in the Fringe systems," she said. "I suppose it will make a few runs to wherever there's trouble."

"I've heard the *Pax* is transporting dignitaries all summer," Kayser said.

"We're taking a new governor to a Fringe World," Dai said.

Kayser asked, "How do you know that?"

Dai shrugged. "I have a Cybot connection. I managed to get him to make a copy of our orders." He reached into his tunic and pulled out a temporary printout and handed it to Aster. "Happy birthday," he whispered so that only she could hear him.

She took the sheet in surprise. "What—?"

"Read it before it evaporates."

The item had the usual slick plastic feel of temporary print-outs. Asteria unfolded it and read the first few lines:

FROM: The Admiralty, RN HQ, Dromia, Corona
TO: Commander C. K. M. Talan, Captain, RNS Pax
You are ordered and charged to convey His Most Royal Highness the Princeps Corinth Kyseros to Central, Theron, where he will take office as Royal Governor—

The document in Asteria's hands vanished like a snowflake landing on a hot stove. She hadn't even finished reading it.

"We're going to Theron!" she said, feeling cold. What if the Bourse demanded her return? Commandant Chen had asked for her trust, but what if—"Theron," Asteria said again, her voice choked.

"Yeah," Dai said. "One of the Empyrator's grandsons is replacing Baron Kamedes as Royal Governor."

"I know all about that," Kayser said. "My uncle told me."

"Rear Admiral Vodros? What does he have to do with it?" Dai asked.

Kayser couldn't keep the superior tone out of his voice. "Plenty. He and the princeps's father were classmates at the Academy. My uncle's in command of Fleet actions in that whole sector. When Kamedes got a promotion to System Director, my uncle recommended the princeps to the post. So the new governor is a friend of my family."

Asteria swallowed. "The commandant must have assigned me to the *Pax* on purpose. I—there are papers I'm supposed to sign on Theron." The thought of being back among the Bourse made her feel queasy.

"Yeah," Dai said. "I'll go with you. I'd like to see your home world."

"I'm sure it's a fascinating place," Kayser said, his voice bland but his sarcasm leaking through.

"After we deliver the Governor," Dai said, pointedly ignoring Kayser, "we're to hang around Theron for a few days for the ceremonies, and then we're to make courtesy calls on all the Fringe Worlds in that sector. They're pretty widely spread, aren't they?"

Asteria nodded. "The closest system is more than twelve light-years away. There are only about five inhabited planets in the whole sector."

"Probably we'll just perform routine patrols, then." Dai paused for several moments and then added, "When, uh, we get to Theron and you take care of, you know, your documents, are you going to spend any time on the surface?"

"Why should I?"

"It's your homeworld."

"Not any longer," she said in such a firm tone that he didn't speak again.

* * *

The *Pax* was already docked at the moon-sized station, undergoing resupply and refitting. Like the *Stinger,* the ship had never been designed for surface landings. Whereas the trainers Asteria had piloted were sleek, black forms, the *Pax* was a thick disk perched atop three cylindrical engine pods. The ship had its own gravigenerators—though because of power drain, the operational gravity of the *Pax* was limited to .75 G, just enough to maintain the crew's muscle tone over months of travel. The cadets presented their credentials to the first mate, Lieutenant Adrio Stensen, who looked almost as young as the graduating seniors.

"Captain's busy," Stensen said after logging them into the ship's system. "We're reconfiguring B deck, so your berths aren't ready yet. We'll arrange for you to stay on station for the next three days or so, and then you can come aboard and receive your assignments."

Their temporary quarters were not much better than the tiny cabin she had occupied on the *Stinger*. Asteria's room smelled stale. One of the lights did not work, and the bed needed a new mattress. On the other hand, she had a small viewport that allowed her a view of Dromia hanging in space.

And she had a little money this time, the Academy's first issue of her small allowance. She treated Dai to a first-class meal in one of the several commercial restaurants on the station and felt astounded to rediscover the fact that food actually had some taste. Even the hydroponic vegetables were better than cadet rations at the Academy. They toured the station too, visiting all the locations available to the public. They watched a commercial transport take off-headed for Coriam, so it carried Aristo passengers. Unlike the battered Fleet vessels Asteria had seen, the liner was sleek and gleaming, a silvery spear that could extrude retractable wings for smooth surface landings.

* * *

The captain of the *Pax,* Commander Talan, was a woman of thirty-five, a little old for such a minor command. Her manner was brusque and businesslike as she handed out assignments. Dai was to serve with AI maintenance and operations; Asteria was to assist the engine crew. The Aristos drew better duties, serving as assistants on the bridge, aides to the officers, or "observers" in stations like astronavigation and weapons systems. Kayser was to act as captain's yeoman, an easy duty. It figured.

Luckily, Asteria found her duties interesting. Lieutenant Skarne, the chief engineer, showed her the setup: the command center, located down on D deck just above the ion-propulsion engines, controlled the grav drive (rarely used, Skarne said, because the ship was only rarely in low orbit), the ion-thrust engines for intrasystem propulsion, and the trans-space drive for FTL. "Think of it this way," Skarne told Asteria. "The trans drive puts us into a secondary universe where we have mass but no dimensions—not in the ordinary sense. Yet every point in the subuniverse corresponds to some location in our time and space. So to take a shortcut between systems, we simply drop into the secondary, then orient ourselves—easy because we have essentially become a point, a singularity—and pop back out at the appropriate spot."

"So travel is instantaneous."

"Subjectively, yes. There's some duration, but it's measured in nanoseconds by ship time. We come back into normal space, make sure of our location—that's where astronavigation comes in—and then either jump again or switch to ion propulsion if we're entering a system." He said, "I suppose you know enough of theory to be able to tell me why we'd jump again?"

"For long journeys," Asteria said promptly. "It's as if there are spots in the subuniverse that don't communicate with each other. You have to go in one way, travel to a different coordinate, and then re-enter the subuniverse to find the final vector to your destination."

"That's about as clear as Varrian slime," Skarne said with a grin. "But I get your meaning." He looked at her. "You know that FTL is dangerous, of course. About one out of every ten thousand jumps destroys the ship."

Asteria nodded. She knew that if the ship rematerialized in a space already occupied by anything with considerable mass—a small asteroid, perhaps, or even another ship—then it couldn't stay together, would explode into a million pieces. Cadets told each other such horror stories all the time, real and made-up.

"There's also another danger this mission," Skarne said seriously. "Tetra probes have been reported in the sector. No battles yet, but we'll go in on high alert." He sighed. "It's frustrating—an enemy you can't negotiate with, can't even talk to. No one knows what the Tetras want or why they're so quick to destroy our ships. Even Raiders will negotiate."

"Yes, sir," Asteria said flatly. She had no interest in negotiating with Raiders.

"Very well. Now, control and operations. I suppose you've checked out on single-pilot trainers?"

"Yes, sir."

"This is completely different. We plug in with control helmets but no pressure suits. This is more cerebral than visceral. You've got to be able to juggle mathematics, physics, and keep on top of about fifty things happening simultaneously. I may be making it sound hard. It's actually harder than I make it sound. I'll let you observe, but you're not going to run the engines any time soon."

"Yes, sir."

"We don't have much to do as long as we're in ion drive. Starting the day after departure, I'll run you though some intensive simulations. If you seem capable, I may let you take a fighter out for a training session eventually. But you'll have to earn that." Skarne's tone softened. "Commoner, are you?"

"Yes, sir, I am," she said.

"So am I. Never make admiral, but so what? They don't have any fun. Keep to Decks B and D unless the captain sends for you to go to the bridge—and hope that doesn't happen, because it would mean you're in trouble. I've looked at your record, Locke. Nice grades, but I find a couple of notes that you have a tendency to insubordination. All right, I don't mind a little insubordination at the appropriate time, but try to keep a lid on it."

"Understood, sir."

"Stand easy. You're a legacy, right?"

"Yes, sir. My father was Carlson Locke."

"And?"

Asteria blinked. She had become so used to her father's being known throughout the Academy that the lieutenant's evident ignorance came as a shock. "Uh—he was on the *Adastra,* sir," she said.

"Oh, right," Skarne said. "Died in the attack?"

"No, sir. He was injured. He died last year on Theron. In a Raider attack."

"I didn't think there had been any Fleet action near Theron."

"He was retired, sir. It didn't involve the Fleet."

Skarne blinked several times, a faint frown drawing his eyebrows. For a moment, Asteria thought he was going to comment, but finally, he just said, "Condolences, Cadet. Well, a year is a long time, but if we find any of those Raiders in the Theron system, we'll try to avenge your father. Don't count on it, though. I've been aboard the *Pax* for seventeen Standard months, and we haven't fired a shot in anger in all that time."

Asteria nodded, her throat tightening.

Skarne opened his mouth and then closed it. After a moment, he sighed. "All right, we're disembarking tomorrow at 1200 ship time. I want you here and in an observing station no later than 1100. Earlier if you want to come earlier. I'll be here. Dismissed."

* * *

The ship buzzed with activity on the day of departure. As Skarne had suggested, Asteria showed up early to take her station— very early. He didn't react, but she had the impression that he was pleased. He installed her in an observer's seat and supplied her with a control helmet, although he explained that he was not activating the controls. "You'll see the readouts and get a sense of what we do," he said, "but you can't affect anything. Just watch and remember."

For an hour before takeoff, the engine crew ran intensive diagnostics, making sure that everything was on line and working at optimal levels. At precisely 1200—in her helmet's visor she could see the time floating in yellow numbers off to the left—the engineers switched from station power to ship power. The readouts dimmed just a bit. Then the engine crew engaged the gravity drive and edged the *Pax* out of its dock. A second readout in red appeared, giving the distance from the space station in kilometers: .050, .85, 1.75...up to 100, when the readout turned green. It was now safe to switch to the ion-thrust drive.

The grav drive shut off silently. A moment later, Asteria felt a subtle shift in her weight as the ion jets cut in, their acceleration pressing her back at half a G. Nothing else changed— no roar, no explosive jerk, nothing. The whole story was told by numbers.

A message addressed to her showed up in bright orange: "Work out a slingshot trajectory that will allow us to exit the system in six days."

"Aye," she replied, and her response showed up in blue.

She activated the calculator and worked at the problem. They could slingshot around Dromia, but that gravity push wouldn't serve their needs. It would take them weeks to move to safe jump distance. There was the possibility of looping around both Dromia and Coriam...more acceleration, but the orbital positions of the two planets were not well placed for such a maneuver...it couldn't be done. The only body in the system that might make it possible was the massive daystar, Corona 2. But they couldn't accelerate to the star in time to—

Wait. She was thinking two-dimensionally, as though it were a trainer problem. They were in space—they could move freely in all three dimensions. So...try this...and this...calculate distances—

She transmitted her solution: slip into a close polar orbit of Dromia, use that to slingshot toward the sun, then loop around the sun's south pole, picking up enough momentum to leave the system at right angles to the plane of orbit…not bad. A little more than six days, but close enough.

A moment later, the chief engineer sent her a pat on the back: *Good work. Your solution is close to what we're going to do.*

Asteria allowed herself a smile. She felt one step closer to becoming a true pilot. One step closer to being able to avenge her father's death herself.

* * *

Aboard the ship, the cadets ate with the junior officers, Aristos and Commoners thrown into the same big cafeteria, but Asteria was still surprised that evening when she saw Dai and Kayser sitting together. She joined them and sat beside Dai. Both of them murmured greetings.

She began to eat, but Kayser said teasingly, "We're not in the Academy, Cadet Locke. We can talk here."

"Nothing to talk about," she said.

Dai told her, "Lord Mastral was saying the Captain is concerned about Tetra ships."

"Shh," Kayser said, glancing around. "It's nothing specific. But we're supposed to come out of FTL at high alert. Kamedes has sent reports in that three monitoring stations have traced plasma residue like the kind Tetra ships leave behind."

"Stellar storms can produce the same kind of plasma traces," Asteria said.

Kayser shrugged. "Well, the captain's taking it seriously, anyway."

Dai took a long sip of cava. "Let's hope there aren't any Tetras around when we drop into normal space," he said. "That's the way they get you. Before you can organize a defense, they come ripping right through your hull."

"We're a warship," Kayser said confidently. "We can take care of them."

Asteria wasn't so sure. She had a really bad feeling about the future. Part of it was worry about going back to Sanctal, even with Dai tagging along. Part of it was her memory of the raid. And now the Tetra threat—

She felt the belt tingle beneath her tunic. Whenever she got worked up, it seemed to engage. It could send her extra stamina, extra energy. It could make her quicker and stronger.

Only—

It couldn't make her less anxious. It couldn't take away her fears about what might lie ahead.

FIFTEEN

One advantage of space travel was that the crew worked watches: ten hours on, fifteen hours off, rotating from day to day. Because Dai and Asteria were both in the aft starboard watch, they had similar schedules. As often as not, Dai wanted to hang out with the AI techies past his watch. Asteria wasn't permitted to do that—there wasn't enough room in Engineering to allow it.

But there were plenty of diversions: she could watch holos of music, drama, history, or science; the gym was always available for a workout; the ship library was extensive and varied. She could occupy herself and put her worries way in the back of her mind, at least temporarily.

Kayser had the same schedule that she and Dai had. He seemed to want to be friends—but Asteria could not bring herself to trust him. They talked occasionally, but they never played games together or shared any secrets. She couldn't allow herself to open up to him; she could barely allow herself to open up to Dai.

Seven days after they had disembarked, the captain warned that the ship was about to jump into FTL drive. It was toward the end of Asteria's watch, and she sat in the observer's seat and saw the switchover to FTL drive occur just before that wrenching sensation of being stretched and turned inside-out made her involuntarily close her eyes for an instant.

And when she opened them, it was over. The ship had popped back into normal space and was angling in for the approach to Theron. The visor display showed the visuals: there was the familiar daystar of the system, and three pinpricks of bright light that had to be the system's three gas giant planets, icy worlds with moons that were large enough and barely warm enough to provide havens for Raiders. Theron itself was too dim and too distant to show up in the display.

Asteria studied the readouts. It would be another ten days before the *Pax* could insert into orbit. A few minutes later, her watch ended, and she surrendered the observer's chair to another midshipman. She walked through the corridors stretching and flexing, working off the stiffness of ten long hours in the seat. To her surprise, she saw Dai coming the other way, excitement on his face. "Come into my room," he said, dissolving the door.

"I don't think that's permitted."

"No one will find out. Come on. I've got something important."

Dai was neater than Asteria. His room was spartan, neat, and so tidy that it hardly looked used. "We'll have to sit on the bed," he said, extruding it from the wall. "Listen, what do you know about Cybots?"

They settled down, side by side. "Cybots?" she asked. "What everyone knows, I guess. They're mechanical, except they're run by neutralized nervous tissue from human donors."

"Neutralized," echoed Dai. "Exactly. They don't retain any memories of when they were alive. No personality. No emotions, because parts of the limbic system are deadened. So Cybots have a kind of human brain, but it's more like—like—"

"A meat computer," Asteria said.

"Uh—yeah. Okay, but sometimes, right, a Cybot has ghost memories. One of the bots on this ship does."

"It remembers its human life?"

"Partial memories. You know how I came aboard at the last minute?"

"Sure."

"Okay, I have a confession. I was able to get a Cybot to change my orders. It had some memory of its former life, and I found out about it. It acknowledged that it had the ghost memories, and it didn't want to give them up—it would be like dying again, I guess. So it agreed to help me—"

"Dai!" exclaimed Asteria. "You blackmailed a Cybot?"

He shook his head. "You make it sound bad! It wasn't like that. When I found out about its memories, it was willing to help. And it did more than get me aboard. It managed to put itself into the rotation too, and it's on the *Pax* now. It's a life-support systems monitor. You've got to talk to it."

Asteria shook her head. "I don't understand. Why?"

"Because it wants to talk to you. It needs to talk to you."

"What do you mean?" Asteria was having a hard time wrapping her mind around that. She thought of Cybots as machines... not as, well, people. "Why?" she asked again.

Dai had been speaking softly; now he dropped his voice to such a soft whisper that Asteria had to lean close to hear his answer. "Because he was on the *Adastra*. Because he knew your father."

* * *

I'm not sure about this.

But here Asteria found herself, forward on B deck, in the life-support control center of the ship. At first, she did not recognize the device in front of her as a Cybot. It had been…dismembered, stripped of arms and legs. It was essentially a quicksilver-shiny torso and egg-shaped head with no features. She could see her own distorted reflection in its face.

Dai was speaking softly into his wrist transceiver. "All right, thanks," he said. He nodded to Asteria. "We're all right. Kayser's in the library. Nobody's monitoring sounds here. We're alone."

The Cybot did not respond, and Asteria licked her lips, which felt dry.

"Speak to him," Dai said.

"I—I'm Asteria Locke," she said hesitantly. "My father was Carlson Locke."

"I served with your father," the Cybot said in its uninflected voice. "I was alive then. Your father was a weapons specialist. I was a weapons engineer. I do not remember my human name."

"I—I'm sorry," Asteria said, feeling the prickle of goose bumps on her arms.

"That has no meaning for me." The Cybot waited silently.

"He can't initiate conversation," Dai said. "You'll have to ask him. Want me to leave?"

"No—no, that's all right. Uh, what did my father do when the Tetraploid attack hit?"

"We operated the weapons. Captain Kyseros was caught without a plan. It is my presumption that the captain panicked under the pressure of the attack. His orders were neither clear nor effective, though he was a princeps of the Aristocracy."

"We've seen how Aristos are always cool under pressure," Dai said sarcastically.

The Cybot seemed to miss his tone completely. "My experience has not shown that to be invariably true. At that time, however, I did place great confidence in our commanding officer. Captain Kyseros did not perform according to my expectations. Even so, and even though we in the weapons crew had to ignore most of his orders, our people fought well. We destroyed seven of the nine attacking Tetra ships."

"Only nine?" Asteria asked.

"Only nine. Very small ships, attacking at extremely close quarters. Nothing like all of our battle simulations. Yet we managed to destroy seven, as I say. The eighth actually impacted the bridge of the *Adastra*. The ninth penetrated the hangar deck where we carried fighters. The enemy ship came apart."

"So it was destroyed too," Asteria said.

"Negative. The ship was not destroyed. It came to pieces and then reassembled as thirty-three spider warriors. They breached the air locks and began an internal assault. Carlson organized a defense, and we defeated the spiders, though we took heavy casualties. Deep scans showed more Tetra ships at a great distance but locked onto us and coming toward us fast. We were receiving no orders. Carlson ascertained that the captain, three of the mates, and most of the bridge crew had been killed when the bridge was destroyed. We could raise no surviving officers on the comm. Therefore, Carlson took command, rerouted navigation and control to his own station, and ordered a retreat. His order was countermanded by...I cannot recall his name...the security officer, a lieutenant and the only officer of rank not dead or badly wounded. He had been hiding. He came out just as Carlson engaged the ion propulsion preparatory to FTL insertion. That officer asserted command, but he was too disorganized to be obeyed."

"What?" Asteria asked, shocked. "I never heard that! I thought my father was the ranking officer when he took command."

"Negative, Asteria Locke. The security officer had not been engaged in the fighting. When he emerged from hiding, he was irrational. He gave Carlson an order to surrender command to him. He wanted to turn and fight, though from the damage we had already sustained, it was clear that the ship would be lost, and the Tetras would then have a wedge into Empyrean space. It was an impasse until I shot the security officer."

"You—*shot* him?" Asteria swallowed hard. Even touching a superior officer was a court-martial offense.

The Cybot's strange, unemotional voice went on: "Affirmative. I shot him with a stunner. He fell, but as he fell, he hit your father with a neural disruptor set at high power. That destroyed the nerve structure in his arm and leg. I tried to apply restraints on the security officer, but a Tetra spider burst into the weapons center. It killed the lieutenant before we could stop it. And it wounded me so severely that Carlson put me in a stasis field to save my life. I remember no more until we reached an Empyrean world and I was removed from the stasis field."

Asteria felt sick. Her father had been part of a mutiny!

"He had to do what he did," Dai said, putting his hand on her shoulder. "By ordering the withdrawal, he saved hundreds of crewmen on the dreadnaught, and by reaching friendly space, he alerted Empyrean forces to the Tetra invasion. But now you see why the Fleet didn't allow him to remain on duty."

Asteria wasn't sure that she did. "Because he didn't surrender command to the lieutenant?"

"Negative," the Cybot said. "Because he knew how ineffective our captain had been. Because he was a Commoner and in time of crisis led the crew better than the Aristo had done. These are facts."

"And your injuries were so bad that they made you a Cybot," Dai said.

"Negative. I was not mortally injured. When I came out of stasis, I told the interrogating officers of what had happened. I mentioned neutralizing the security lieutenant. His family demanded my death. I was killed at their request, and my brain was harvested for Cybot creation. I do not know why all my memories were not purged."

"That's horrible!" blurted Asteria.

"That has no meaning to me," the Cybot said.

Appalled, Asteria thought: *It doesn't even resent the terrible things that were done to it—to him! It can't feel anger or resentment. Its humanity has been stolen.*

And the same thing could have happened to her father. She turned and blundered out. Behind her the Cybot hummed softly, probably monitoring air quality. Dai hurried after her. "I thought you should know," he said, sounding upset. "The new Governor we're taking to Theron is in the same branch of the royal family as the captain of the *Adastra* was. Of course, there are about a million in the Kyseros branch, so—hey, come on. What's the matter?"

"I don't—I never thought—I'm sorry. I want to be alone," Asteria stammered.

The Cybot wanted to tell me, she thought. *It has nothing human left to it—nothing but a few scattered memories. And if the memories die, the last connection of that mind to its old life dies. It told me because it wanted to show that it still had that one shred of humanity left.*

And because I'm my father's daughter.

She felt too nauseated even to think of eating. There had been times at the Academy when she had questioned the privileges claimed by Aristos. Now she'd learned the awful truth about an incompetent Aristo captain and an irrational Aristo lieutenant who had tried to prevent Carlson Locke's saving the survivors of the *Adastra*. The Fleet's judgment was that the incompetent and the irrational should have been obeyed—they were Aristos, and Carlson Locke had been a Commoner. Just like his daughter. And like Lieutenant Skarne, she could never hope to make Admiral.

What's the point? Asteria knew how good she was—and knew, too, that no matter how hard she tried, there would always be someone like Kayser in her way. With the money on deposit for her, she could find something to do. Commercial piloting, maybe, or even farming. She knew farming. Despised it but knew it.

Her father had never intended her for the Academy. He had wanted to send her cousin instead.

He must have known. Any child of Carlson Locke would be marked. Aristos who knew the truth would have it in for her.

Kayser had said that the new governor of Theron was an old family friend. And his uncle, Admiral Vodros, was close to the new governor's father.

No wonder Vodros had tried to get her thrown out of the Academy. Asteria began to feel as though she were caught in a web. And the spiders were Aristos.

She pondered for far too long, got far too little sleep, and the next watch found her groggy and inattentive. Skarne took her aside and asked, "Are you sick?"

"No," she said. "Just tired."

"Take off, then," he said. "It's just ion running, and there's nothing much to it. Get some rest. That's an order."

She shambled away, still feeling disoriented and off-kilter, and found herself wandering to the nav center, where she studied the display. The *Pax* had penetrated the Theron system, and now the outer gas giant showed clearly as a planet, its pale yellow disk streaked with red and orange lines. A few more days and then they would be at the High Docks. As soon as she got shore leave, she would arrange the final transfer of the credits she had inherited, and then if she chose, she could announce her resignation from the Academy and set about finding some place for herself.

But she wouldn't. It didn't matter if the whole Aristocracy stood against her. She had something to do, something to prove, if only to herself.

Asteria entered her room and instantly felt a jolt of energy.

The belt pulsed, shocked her into heightened awareness.

There—on her bunk—

It swooped into the air and dived toward her, a machine, a little maintenance bot—

She sidestepped and ducked, and it crashed into the bulkhead just behind her, hard enough to have fractured her skull if it had hit. It whirred angrily and rebounded from the wall. No room to fight, too tight in here—

She elbowed the door control, but the door remained solid. The bot, the size of her head, sizzled toward her again.

She raised her arms in an X block, knowing she'd probably suffer cracked bones—

The belt somehow had flowed upward, had coated both of her arms in metal—she saw her silver hands—

In slow motion, the bot hurtled toward her—

She locked her hands and brought them down hard in a double-hammer blow.

This is crazy, I'll break every bone—

She struck the bot, and it smashed to the floor, dented and disabled. Smoke curled out of it.

Asteria dropped to the floor, grasped the bot along a seam, and ripped. Her silvered fingers had enormous strength. She peeled back the metal cover, reached in, and smashed the activator circuitry. The bot died.

Breathing hard, Asteria stood on shaky legs. The bot, now just a small chunk of wreckage, sent a last wisp of smoke into the air.

The door vanished, responding late.

Asteria raised her communicator and said, "Security!"

No response. The flowing metal from the belt had coated the communicator—

The bot crumpled in on itself and fumed away to nothing.

No evidence.

Asteria quickly inspected her room. No other surprises.

But someone had programmed a repair-and-welding unit to attack her. Someone wanted her dead.

Kayser?

Who else could it be?

Asteria closed and sealed the door and then sank onto her bunk. The silver ebbed from her fingers as the belt reabsorbed the coating of metal.

So, she thought. The Tetras weren't the only enemy. Or the Raiders.

And who could she tell? Not Security—she had no proof that anything had happened. The bot had not even dented the tough bulkhead. Not Command—the captain was under the direct supervision of Princeps Kyseros, a high-ranking Aristo. Not even—not even Dai.

Because if he knew, he could be a target too.

She would have to go it alone, trust only herself, and be vigilant, if she wanted to graduate, if she wanted to become a pilot.

If she wanted to live.

SIXTEEN

The *Pax* could not raise the High Docks on communications. Nor could it reach any transmitter on the surface of Theron. "Something's interfering," Asteria heard a communications officer say in the mess room. "Maybe it's solar activity, but I've never known any this bad."

The engine crew seemed worried. Following the captain's orders, they dropped into unusually high orbit, fifty kilometers from the docks. Under visual magnification, everything looked intact—but there was no space traffic at all, unusual for a docking station. No ships orbited near, no large craft were visible in the three big docks.

In Engineering, Skarne said to Asteria, "The princeps wants to be ferried down to the surface in a lander. I don't think that's wise myself—not without communications. But he wants to assume his post. The captain wants him to have an honor guard, so we're sending six fighters to accompany him." He tilted his head. "Want to be the seventh?"

"Me? Pilot a fighter?"

"I thought you'd like to try a real ship after those trainers," Skarne said with a grin. "If you'll promise not to accidentally discharge your weapons, you can fly as the rear guard. You are not to land on the surface, though; once the others have safely landed, you are to return to post. Clear?"

Asteria felt her heart pumping hard at the thought of flying again. Skarne was smiling at her. She thought, *he has all the skills to reprogram a repair bot—but he's a Commoner.*

Commoners could be bribed.

"How about it?" Skarne asked.

"Sure," Asteria told him. "Thanks. But why did you pick me?"

"Because you're a good pilot," Skarne said. "Because the fighter controls are almost identical to the trainers you did so well on. And because you're a Commoner. We don't get many chances."

Still wondering if Skarne was her friend, Asteria reported to the fighter bay and paused to admire the sleek craft. Like the Cybots, they looked almost like liquid mercury, teardrops of shining metal just large enough to accommodate a pilot. They were reliable, responsive vessels.

Unless one had been reprogrammed to be a death trap.

With her nerves fluttering, she suited up, put on the helmet, and fell into the adopted habit of not breathing as the suit fed her oxygen. The six real pilots didn't even acknowledge her—all Aristos, she thought, though she could not see cheek tattoos through the visors and did not ask. They stood at attention while Captain Talan, her face unusually grim, escorted the slender, dark-haired Princeps Corinth Kyseros—he didn't look old enough to be given command of a planet—and his entourage to a lander, a shuttle capable of ferrying fifteen people to the surface.

The pilots manned their craft, and Asteria felt the familiar tingle of anticipation as the ship merged with and enhanced her senses. Quickly, she did an especially thorough check of all systems, then ran three sets of diagnostics. All seemed to be in order.

The flight deck was cleared. The huge air lock was opened, and the first two fighters moved out under grav drive, followed by the shuttle, then two more fighters, two more, and finally Asteria's ship.

Her heart swelled as she sailed into the silence of space. Theron hung in the velvet blackness, glowing blue, shining white, beautiful. Stars gleamed unblinking. The High Docks sailed ahead, a complicated and intricate structure that looked as though it had been put together haphazardly.

The commlink cut in: "Guard seven, when you're within range, close with the docking station and give it a visual inspection."

"Aye," Asteria subvocalized. She made a face. Now she knew why she had been given the chance to accompany the new governor. There was a job to do that no Aristo wanted! Typical.

Guard one gave the command to switch to ion propulsion, and the shuttle and its escorts began to move rapidly away from the *Pax*. Their trajectory would take them within a kilometer or so of the High Docks. It did not need to be a long detour, Asteria decided.

She peeled off as the flight made its nearest approach to the docks. She reported in: "The station's lights are on. I see no activity in the docks at all. I see six, eight small craft moored." She scanned the station as her fighter moved within mere meters of its outer hull. "I read power activity in the normal range. I don't see any—"

Ahead the hull of the Docks' main repair bay exploded silently, a blast of orange flame and gas. Before Asteria could react, she felt the belt beneath her pressure suit expand, and then she dropped into the strange slow-motion perception. Amid the boiling vapors from the ragged hole in the station's hull, she saw darting shapes: a cloud of deadly silver craft shaped like broad arrowheads. "Raider ships!" she transmitted. "Twenty or more, fighter-class!"

She received no acknowledgment. Something was jamming communications.

Three of the silvery Raider fighters had angled away from the cloud of ships that had erupted from the Docks. They peeled off toward her. She saw the sudden gleam of plasma cannon, rolled, half-looped, and turned, pulling high G forces as she fled toward the governor's flight—still in formation, apparently unaware of danger. "Alert!" she transmitted, forgetting to subvocalize, actually yelling the word. She regained control: "Alert! We're under attack!"

No response. She was barely ahead of the enemy fighters. Why weren't they firing?

Of course—plasma bolts would get the attention of the Empyrean pilots!

And she fired a warning shot. Saw it sizzle past the portside escorts. Saw them suddenly break formation.

She whipped her fighter around and closed with an enemy craft. Her targeting sensors went out.

They're jamming our tech!

She had targeted visually before, in the War Games back at the Academy. The enemy ship fired a plasma bolt at the same instant she fired her laser cannon at it. She rolled the fighter, and the shot missed her by a matter of half a meter or less.

But she scored a direct hit. The enemy fighter blossomed into gas and debris.

She had no time to think, no time to plan. Now she could see the *Pax*, far away—and she could see the glowing green trace lines of ion exhaust from dozens of fighters closing in. *Wake up! Fight back!*

A spear of white leaped from the *Pax*. One of the fighters closest to it exploded. The flight deck hatch dissolved, and she could just make out a swarm of Empyrean fighters exiting the *Pax*. Then her 360-degree vision caught an enemy ship sailing into position to fire at her, and she reversed thrust just as its laser flared. The laser beam passed through the space she had been occupying a half-heartbeat before.

They took the High Docks! The Raiders took the High Docks and are using it as their base!

She saw impacts and explosions as the enemy fighters concentrated their fire on the *Pax*. A cruiser had good shielding, and a fighter couldn't hope to penetrate it—not one fighter alone.

Twenty-five or thirty was a different matter. But what Raider would attack an Empyrean ship? That was madness—the government might overlook a random raid on a Fringe World, but a direct attack was different.

Asteria Locke.

The comm was working again! "Here! A flight of thirty to fifty Regus-class fighters—"

They are not piloted by humans.

"Who's this?"

I do not remember my name.

The Cybot!

"Alert the Captain!"

Already done. I cannot communicate with our fighters. Only with you. Seek out a faceted orb. That will be the Tetra command vessel. Destroy the orb.

197

Tetras! Here, in the Theron system!

An enormous explosion planetside. Asteria's throat tightened. The shuttle had been destroyed. She closed with an enemy fighter, fired, did some damage, whisked past it. Then she was in the midst of a swarm of them. Her mind buzzed with a cross-chatter of bizarre, inhuman voices, overlapping each other—

Move to seize the main craft. Take the main craft.

Acknowledged.

Acknowledged.

The small craft is an easy target.

No, follow the Admiral's orders and concentrate on seizing the main craft.

Acknowledged.

Asteria gasped. The communications were not coming through her commlink—nor were they expressed in words. It was more like a direct flow of thought, so intense that for a moment she felt a fierce urge to join the enemy fighters, to attack the *Pax*.

Seize the main craft.

The Admiral's orders.

She had a searing vision of Theron being scoured clean of human life.

Sterilize.

She felt an alien resentment that the Admiral was one of them, was human, and that the Admiral's orders must be obeyed.

The main craft. Take the main craft—

They wanted to take the cruiser. As they had taken the Raider fighters. The Tetras wanted a cruiser—

Or the one giving the orders wanted them to take it. What admiral would give such an order?

The *Adastra* had been a dreadnaught, but even so, nine small Tetra craft attacking without warning had all but destroyed it. If the Tetras had command of a cruiser—

Find the orb!

"How am I receiving the Tetra transmissions?"

Unknown. We have sustained damage. Someone aboard is disrupting all communications. Hurry! Find the orb!

Someone aboard.

Kayser. It had to be Kayser! Whose uncle was an admiral—

Asteria's trajectory had taken her past the High Docks. She saw two Empyrean fighters ahead, confronting three enemies. She accelerated to help, and at extreme range, she fired, disabling one of the enemy ships. As her fighter flashed past it, she concentrated fiercely: *Where is the orb?*

And she felt a surge of—not emotion, too diffuse to be called that—an urge, an irrational desire, to protect the orb—to keep it safe—alien minds thinking of the orb, thinking of its position—

It's under the Docks!

Garbled transmissions now: "They've retreated!"

"They're attacking the *Pax*. Guard flight, report in! Who's with us? Guard one here!"

"Guard three!"

Silence. Asteria said, "Guard seven! Come with me. There's a Tetra ship near the High Docks. Concentrate your fire on that!"

She soared away without hearing any acknowledgment. Ahead, above, lay the High Docks, and past it the *Pax,* now fighting desperately. The Docks swelled rapidly in her view as she sped toward it, recklessly using the ship's energy. If she didn't have enough left to get back to the *Pax* or enough to engage the enemy command ship, it wouldn't matter anyway.

There it was! Nearly invisible, a jet-black, glittering, faceted orb, only tens of meters across. It was already firing missile weapons, tiny streaking lances less than a meter long. Asteria waited until they were moments away, then switched on grav drive, set to its highest level. The repelling force pulsed outward, and the incoming missiles glanced off the invisible barrier. Now the orb was firing lasers—and again she had the uncanny sense of hearing the enemy communications:

Fighters protect the command. Command under attack by two enemies. Fighters protect the command.

Two? With a sickening lurch, Asteria realized that Guard one had been destroyed. She fired her plasma cannon. The orb twirled, and she missed; but she had locked onto the target visually, and with her heightened instincts, she maneuvered to keep it in sight, the G forces all but pulling her apart. Six enemy fighters vectoring in fast. Now the orb was against the blue of Theron, a stark black shape.

You cannot do this. We have allied with the human command. You cannot do this—

"Watch me," she said aloud, and she loosed every weapon she had. The orb exploded, and a moment later, her fighter plunged through the wreckage, taking hits. She felt—

Ours! Ours! Our—

The belt.

Tetra technology!

That was how she had intercepted their communications—

But it was no longer Tetra tech. It had molded itself to her physiology, to her mind—

Everything went black.

SEVENTEEN

She floated in absolute darkness. The fighter had taken damage. Its sensors no longer worked. She had no power. No life support.

I've got maybe five minutes of oxygen. My last trajectory will take me straight into the atmosphere of Theron. The fighter will burn up on entry. So—I'll suffocate, or I'll burn. Which will happen first?

She had barely had time to think that before she felt the weird sensation that the belt was growing again. But this time—

This time, it didn't stop.

It flowed up her body and down her legs. She had no way of judging time. It could have taken a nanosecond, or it could have taken a full minute.

She couldn't resist, not in the pressure suit, not locked into the body-contoured confines of the fighter. Not when the flowing metal encased her face. Not when it closed over her head, over her fingers, over her toes, completely armoring her body.

And then—

Then she saw.

Not with her eyes, but through the skin of living metal that had covered her. She saw through the fighter itself, a universe sketched in unfamiliar colors and pulsing with unknown energies. Theron spun before her. The fighter was almost at the edge of the atmosphere. She had seconds left to live—

But another craft was pacing her. It was not a fighter, but a repair unit, moving too fast for its systems. It extruded claspers.

It can't possibly have enough power to lift the fighter.

She felt rather than heard the sound, transmitted through the fighter hull, of the pincers seizing the fighter. And then the hatch crumpled away.

"Aster! Are you alive?"

Dai.

"Here," she subvocalized. "I'm here!"

She *felt* the armor transmit the words in the comm spectrum.

"Can you get out? I think your pressure suit might have half a minute of oxygen left."

"I'll try."

She braced herself and shoved. The crumpled hatch broke free and tumbled away. She pushed herself out of the pilot's cradle—and felt the ripping of the pressure suit. It shredded away.

But the armor held. She writhed into space, reached for a handhold, and seized the pincers. "I'm holding onto your ship. Let the fighter go, or we'll both be dragged down!"

The pincers opened, and the repair ship powered up. "Can you hang on? I'll have to try to pull you inside!"

"Negative!" cried Asteria. "Lift us out with grav drive! I'll let you know if I'm running out of air, then we can worry about getting me aboard!"

She locked her arms through the struts of the pincer. Between her dangling feet, she saw her fighter, mangled, twirling down toward the planetary surface. Only when it had begun to streak orange did she say, "Are we in safe orbit?"

"For the moment. All right, I'm going to open the retrieval bay. I think I can route oxygen into it. Hang on!"

Behind her, the bay hatch dissolved. She hauled herself inside. "Close it!"

The bay hatch reformed. "How's your ox?" Dai asked anxiously.

"No readings."

"Flooding the bay…pressurized. Can you take off your helmet?"

It was a tight fit. She squirmed and twisted and finally managed to unseal and take off the flight helmet. Her face was still encased in the metal armor that had formed from the belt. "Helmet's off," she said, without mentioning the armor. "What's happening on the *Pax*?"

"The enemy fighters broke off contact. They're dead in space now. Our fighters are mopping up. Talan's sent a marine detachment to retake the Docks. How did Raiders get so many ships?"

"From the Tetras," Asteria told him grimly. "They've been capturing Empyrean ships for years. We were wrong about the Tetras. They're not organic. They're something like living machines. Silicon-based. They don't think we're real."

"What?"

"They see us as something like Cybots. But that's changed. Someone in the Fleet has allied with them. Some kind of bargain—the Tetras want this system. I saw their minds. They want to—to sterilize Theron, to kill all life on it. I don't know why."

"The planet's all right. We've established contact. The jamming broke off all of a sudden. They've been cut off because all the orbiting stations were seized a few days ago, but the population's all right." A pause, and then Dai added, "We lost the new governor."

"I saw it happen."

"Okay, we're coming up to the ship. This is going to be a rough landing. A lot of systems are down. Hang on."

It was a very rough landing. But the armor that encased Asteria somehow anticipated every jolt and twist, and it spurred her to brace an arm, stiffen a leg, and hang on for dear life. And at last, just before the bay door dissolved again, the armor retreated, flowed down her body, and became a belt again.

She crept out onto a flight deck that showed the shambles of battle. Dai hopped out of the repair pod's cockpit. He held out a hand and helped her up. She remembered to breathe again—the armor had taken over the job of supplying oxygen to her, having "learned" that from the pressure suit—and gasped, "How bad?"

"We lost fourteen of our fifty fighters," Dai said. "Took hull and structural damage. Lost about half of our sensor array. We had casualties aboard too. I don't know how many."

Asteria saw a familiar face in the crowd on the flight deck. Kain Kayser came toward them, a look of concern on his thin face. "Are you two all right?"

"We're fine," Asteria said. "Where were you in the fighting?"

"Me?" Kayser blinked. "I—I was helping, trying to regain communications—"

"Funny how everything went dead at the crucial moment."

Kayser's eyes narrowed. "We were doing all we could," he said. "But I'm glad you two are safe." He held out a hand to Dai. "They'll call you a hero for going out in a repair ship to rescue her."

Dai ignored his hand. "No, they won't," he said. "I did it without orders. I stole the ship."

"Get to stations!" an officer yelled, and they split up.

In the engine control room, Asteria learned that the engine crew had not lost anyone. "We were working overtime, though," Skarne said. "The weapons had a high energy demand."

"What happens on Theron now that the designated governor is dead?" Asteria asked him.

"Don't know. I expect that the planet will be placed under military rule. It's the first Tetra engagement in this sector, so everything will be on high alert. There will probably be a military governor."

"Who?" Asteria asked.

Skarne shrugged. "Admiral Vodros is the ranking officer in this sector. Why are you so curious?"

"It used to be my home," Asteria told him.

EIGHTEEN

It took Empyrean Marines a day to recapture the High Docks. The survivors on the Docks told what they knew:

A Raider group based on one of the moons of Cyclad, the first gas giant in the system, had encountered the faceted orb that was in fact a Tetra command ship. Its method still was not clear, but it had enslaved them, used them to pilot a collection of human fighter craft that the Tetras had accumulated. And under the direction of the Tetra command ship, the humans had captured all of the orbital stations around Theron.

And waited...for an Empyrean warship.

"This is a new phase of war," Captain Talan announced to the crew. "Reinforcements will be here soon. In the meantime, Theron is under military government. Admiral Vodros will be here in a few days to take command. Until then, we're on guard duty. Before the admiral arrives, we have to make sure that the Tetra influence did not reach the surface."

* * *

That afternoon, Talan sent for Asteria, and she reported to the bridge. The captain told her to stand at ease and said, "I understand you attacked and destroyed the Tetra command craft," she said.

"Aye, Captain."

Talan shook her head. "A capture would have been much better. It would have given us a chance to analyze and understand their technology."

Asteria felt a pulse of anger. "It was a battle, Captain. I was doing my best."

"A Fleet pilot has to think fast, Cadet."

Kayser was looking at them. Asteria thought of her suspicions—that Kayser had sabotaged communications, that his uncle had somehow set up the attack—but she had no proof, no proof at all.

And she was a Commoner.

"I will try to remember that in the future, Captain," she said, quivering inside with frustration and fury.

Talan gazed at her for a long moment. "Very well. As you said, you had little time. And then we did defeat the Tetra force. I will note in the official battle report that you served as an emergency fighter pilot and that you lost your craft in the battle, but will also note that you fought well. Do you have anything to say?"

Yes! The Fleet is in danger from one of its own officers!

Asteria bit back the words. Aloud, she said, "No, Captain."

"Dismissed."

* * *

Who should she trust? Who could she trust?

It came down to Dai.

On the day when two more cruisers dropped into orbit, she told him what she knew.

"There must be some way of proving this," Dai said.

"None. But someone reprogrammed a bot to try to kill me. Someone destroyed the main comm circuitry just as the enemy fighters broke out of the High Docks."

"Kayser."

"I don't know. I think so, but—I don't know."

"And now his uncle is in control of the whole sector. We have to tell someone."

"Who?"

Dai shook his head. "I don't know…"

"We have to wait," Asteria said. "It's going to be hard, but we're going to have to find people we can trust, let them in on the secret. Make sure more people know so if something happens to us—"

"But it's crazy. Who would ally with the Tetras? For what?"

"Control of the Empyrion, maybe," Asteria said.

Dai gave her a sick look. "They're Aristos," he said in a whisper. "But they're human!"

Asteria said, "I—I don't know what to call it—I plugged in to the Tetra mind somehow. I think it was the belt. But, Dai, I saw how they feel about us. They don't even know we're alive! Not in the same way they are. And I think they ran into an Aristo who feels that way too. We don't matter. People don't matter. Just—just power and control."

"He has to be stopped," Dai said.

"But we can't do it alone," Asteria said. "Not yet. So we have to stick it out. We have to go back to the Academy, make our way up through the ranks, and one day—one day we'll have our chance."

"If we live," Dai said with a grin.

Asteria took a long, deep breath. The belt felt strangely heavy, a burden almost too great to bear.

"Yes," she said. "If we live."

the adventure continues
in the next book of
the academy series

✳ ✳ ✳

Even the underpowered practice weapons had to be handled carefully. As quartermaster for the team, Asteria had the responsibility of checking in the side arms and storing them following every practice session. It was a routine task, but she had to be attentive. Each cadet in the section had to turn over his or her weapon, stunners or disruptors or missile guns, to Asteria. In turn, she had to deactivate each, log it in, and see that it was properly stored. It usually took her half an hour to get everything done, and then she would have to dash to Tactics—each time a cadet was late, the teacher handed out five demerits.

On the seventh day of the week, just before End Break, Asteria had depowered all twenty-five stunners. As usual, that did not take very long, even though not all cadets were as enthusiastic as Kayser—his weapons always came back drained, needing only a quick check and deactivation. Most had to be powered down, which could take a few seconds.

Asteria checked the time and saw she was cutting it close. The last thing she needed this week was five more demerits. Last stunner done. Good. She placed it on the cart with the others and then pushed the hovercart to the weapons storage vault, opened the shield door—it had to be blast-resistant so it was a heavy five-layered durosteel and flexal construction—and then took a deep breath. Her claustrophobia always bothered her when she first stepped into the vault. She shoved the hovercart ahead of her, pushed it to the set of drawers that her class used for storage, and unlocked tray 11. The drawer slipped smoothly out of the back wall. Then each stunner had to be fitted into the correct recessed holder, from 11-1 to 11-25. Only when that had been done and the AI had scanned them to make sure they were deactivated would the drawer slide closed and the tray lock re-engage.

Because the narrow vault made her feel so uneasy, Asteria was hurrying, maybe concentrating a little too hard on the task. Behind her the door slammed, taking her completely by surprise. The light went out. Nothing is as dark as the inside of an unlighted vault.

Her first wild thought was that the door had simply swung closed on its own. It was heavy but delicately balanced on its hinges, and sometimes it would swing a little if you hadn't opened it all the way. She held up her arm and commanded, "Light," and her wrist communicator gave her a pale blue beam. She touched the storage drawer; it slipped back into place, and the red "locked" light glowed briefly to confirm that the weapons were secure and accounted for.

Then Asteria, breathing a little too fast, tried to turn the release wheel to open the vault door.

It stuck.

Someone had locked the vault door from outside.

Kayser? Or—someone else?

Now Asteria was gasping for air. She knew that it was just a panic reaction. There was plenty of oxygen in the vault, enough for hours. But this was like her nightmares, like being stranded in the darkness inside the disabled fighter ship back at Theron. Her heart was thudding fast. Being closed in was the one thing she could not stand.

Her voice shaky, she keyed the comm line to Emergency and said, "Cadet A. F. Locke here. I'm locked inside the side arms vault in the Quartermaster Unit. I need immediate help. Any Academy personnel respond. I need help."

No response. Gasping, beginning to sweat, Asteria realized that someone had not only locked her in but had also turned on the vault's electromagnetic shielding. It was designed to prevent AI scans of the facility, just in case some bright student wanted to borrow a weapon and needed the combinations, but it also damped out communications.

They'll come looking for me, Asteria told herself. Dai and the others knew her routine. It might take a few hours, but they would come to check on her. If she didn't go crazy from claustrophobia first. She tried to take deep breaths, to calm herself—

Without warning, she felt the belt begin to flow over her skin. "No!"

But she couldn't stop it or control it. The quicksilver metal encased her in moments, and the humming, maddening Tetra voices whispered just below the threshold of comprehension. Cold and inhuman voices. And she couldn't understand a syllable, though she had a paranoid sense that they were aware of her, were seeking her.

But with the silver mask completely covering her face, at least she could see. The armor converted infrared and ultraviolet to visible shapes. She could make out the vault, a wide room six meters from side to side but only a meter and a half deep, in cold blues and purples. The pulsing dull red lines of shielding crept and writhed over the walls and doors. A humming crackle of electromagnetic energy muttered in her ears, overpowering the voices. She felt an urgent tug at her attention.

Off to the left in the back wall, one whole drawer glowed a brilliant yellow.

Power. The weapons in the drawer are fully powered.

Asteria felt a jolt of adrenaline. Something was very wrong.

She stepped to the wall of storage compartments and entered the code, and the glowing drawer slid noiselessly open just below chest level. On the tray lay twenty-five Keeler stunners, used by the senior classes and quite a bit more powerful than the ones her classmates were allowed. They shimmered with orange white power, looking like metal heated to the melting point.

With a shock, Asteria saw that the energy cells were looping, their power circuits resonating and thrumming. They were ready to—

Explode.

And even though the silver armor gave her some protection, if twenty-five stunners blew up in this contained space, she would be dead.

Moving faster than she would have thought possible, Asteria snatched one of the stunners from its recess and keyed it down, dropped it, reached for a second one, switched it off before the first had hit the deck, reached for a third—

Even moving at incredible speed she wouldn't be able to turn them all off.

Someone had trapped her.

Someone wanted her dead.

about the author

Brad Strickland is the author of more than fifty novels for teen-agers and young readers, including the popular John Bellairs mystery series and the critically acclaimed Mars: Year One series. Several of his books have been honored by the New York Public Library's Best Books for the Teen Age list, and he is a past Georgia Author of the Year and an honoree of the Junior Library Guild. His books have been translated into eighteen foreign languages. When he's not dreaming up stories, Brad teaches English at Gainesville State College in Georgia. He and his wife, Barbara, (who sometimes co-writes with him) have two grown children, Jonathan and Amy, and three cats and two dogs—a full house.